THE BESTSELLING SERIES
CONTINUES
WITH A BOLD NEW ADVENTURE!

"A continuously growing series of talented young SF authors . . . these books are really quite remarkable . . . the series promises to be well-received by Asimov fans."

—*Thrust*

"Like the movie serials of old, the publisher has me hooked, and I'll be watching the stands . . ."

—Mark Sabljak,
Milwaukee Journal

ISAAC ASIMOV'S ROBOT CITY™
ROBOTS AND ALIENS

Alliance by Jerry Oltion

A Byron Preiss Visual Publications, Inc. Book

ACE BOOKS, NEW YORK

This book is an Ace original edition, and has never been previously published.

ISAAC ASIMOV'S ROBOT CITY
ROBOTS AND ALIENS
BOOK 4: ALLIANCE

An Ace Book/published by arrangement with Byron Preiss Visual Publications, Inc.

PRINTING HISTORY
Ace edition/May 1990

ISBN: 0-441-73130-9

Ace Books are published by the Berkley Publishing Group,
200 Madison Avenue, New York, New York 10016.
The name ''Ace'' and the ''A'' logo are trademarks belonging to
Charter Communications, Inc.

PRINTED IN THE UNITED STATES OF AMERICA

10 9 8 7 6 5 4 3 2 1

CONTENTS

ROBOTS AND FATHERS
ISAAC ASIMOV

All of us began as fertilized ova, obviously. For the first nine months, or maybe a little less, we existed in a womb which, under normal conditions, represents about as close to total security as we are likely ever to have. Unfortunately, we have no way of knowing and appreciating this security at that time.

We are then brought suddenly into the outside world, with a certain amount of violence, and are exposed, for the first time, to changes in temperature, to the rough touch of moving air, to breathing, drinking and eliminating only with effort (however instinctive and automatic that effort might be). The womb is forever gone.

Nevertheless, each of us, if we have had a normal infancy, has parents; a mother, in particular, who labors to substitute for the womb as much as possible. We are all nearly help-less, but mothers and, to some extent, fathers, if enlight-ened, see that we are warm, comfortable, fed, washed, dried, and given a chance to sleep undisturbed. It is still not bad, and we are still in no condition to appreciate our good fortune.

Then comes the stage when we are aware of our surroundings. Still small, still largely helpless, we become able to understand the dangers that on us press; we become capable of feeling fear and panic; we become able to grasp, however dimly, the discomfort of loss or threatened loss, and the anguish of unfulfilled desire.

Even then, there is a means of relief and redress. There are the looming figures of father and mother (and, to a far lesser extent, older siblings, if any). We have all seen young children clinging to a father's leg desperately, or peeping out from behind a mother's clutched skirt at the fearful sight of other human beings or almost any other kind of novel experience. We see them (and perhaps we can think of ourselves in the dim earliest memories we have) rushing to mother or father as the all-encompassing security.

I remember my daughter, Robyn, at the comparatively advanced age of fourteen, telling me how she had taken an airplane under threatening weather conditions. When I registered fear and terror at what might have been the consequences, she said, calmly, "I wasn't afraid, because Mamma was with me and I knew she wouldn't allow anything to happen to me."

And when she was nineteen, she was temporarily marooned in Great Britain's Heathrow airfield because of a "work action." She called me long distance (collect) to tell me of her sad plight and said, with sublime confidence, "Do something!" I was about to try when they announced her plane was taking off and I did not have to reveal my inability to move mountains.

It is inevitable, however, that all children reach the stage where they realize that their parents are but human beings and are not creatures of ultimate ability and wisdom. Most children learn it a lot sooner than mine did because I went to considerable pains to play the role.

Whenever children learn of their parents' fallibility and weakness, there is bound to be a terrible feeling of loss. The loss is so intense that there is an inevitable search for a substitute, but where can you find it?

Primitive man naturally argued by analogy. If human beings can puff their breath outward, then the wind (an enormous puff of breath) must be the exhalation of a vast supernatural being like a human being but immensely larger and more powerful, a windgod. By similar arguments, an incredible array of supernatural entities were built up—an entire imaginary Universe.

To begin with, it was assumed that these supernatural beings were as contentious, as irascible, as illogical, as passion-ridden as were the human beings on whom they were modeled. They had to be placated endlessly, flattered, praised and bribed into behaving kindly. It was, I suppose, a great advance when the idea arose that a supernatural being might be naturally kind, merciful and loving, and would *want* to help and cherish human beings.

And when that happened, human beings at last found the father they had lost as they grew up—not the actual, fallible, human father who might still be alive (and a fat lot of good he was), but the superhuman, all-encompassing, all-knowing, all-powerful father they had had as an infant.

Thus, in the Sermon on the Mount, Jesus repeatedly refers to "your Father which is in heaven." Of course, it might be argued that the term "Father" is used metaphorically, rather than literally, but metaphors are not developed without reason.

"Fathers" are also found at lower levels than that of a supreme God, since the search for lost security can move in many directions. The representatives of God on Earth may get the title, too. "Pope" is a form of the word "Papa" (it *is* "papa" in Italian), which is a common word for "father" in many Indo-European languages. And lest the point be lost, he is also called "the Holy Father." Roman Catholic priests and High Church Episcopalian priests are also addressed as "Father."

The early theological scholars of the Catholic Church are called "the Fathers of the Church." It is even possible to look at certain purely secular individuals who are regarded with particular veneration in that fashion. We speak of the "Pilgrim Fathers," for instance.

We lend the name to Earthly abstractions, too. If one is particularly sentimental about one's place of birth, its land, its customs, its culture, how can one better describe it than as the "Fatherland." The Germans have done so with such assiduity and so loudly ("Vaterland") that the word has come to mean Germany, in particular, and that has made it hard for other nations to use it. We can still speak of the "Motherland" or the "Mother Country," however. The feminine symbolism bespeaks not so much the sword and spear as the flowing breasts—so perhaps "Motherland" is the healthier metaphor.

The words for "father" and "mother" show up as metaphors in hidden form (for us) because they lurk behind Greek and Latin. The rulers of Rome were the surrogate "fathers" of the State (and pretty lousy and selfish fathers they were). They were "patricians" from the Latin word "pater," meaning "father." From "pater," we also get the Latin word for "fatherland," so that now we know what a "patriot" is.

A Greek city often sent out colonists who founded other cities which were, essentially, independent, but which often harbored a sentimental attachment for "the mother-city." The Greek word for city is "polis" and for mother is "meter." The mother-city is therefore the "metropolis." Nowadays, the name is used for any large city dominating a region and the thought is lost—but it's there.

But has any of this anything to do with robots which are, after all, the subject of my introductions to the series of novels which are brought together under the generic title of "Robot City"?

Surely you can guess. To use mathematical terminology: parent is to child as human being is to robot.

Suppose we rephrase the Three Laws of Robotics and have it the Three Laws of Children, instead.

The First Law would read: *A child must not do harm to its parents or, by inaction, allow its parents to come to harm.*

One of the Ten Commandments is that we must honor our father and our mother. When I was brought up (by immigrant parents steeped in Talmudic lore), doing my parents harm was unthinkable and, believe me, the thought never occurred to me. In fact, even being impudent was a terrible thing that would have blackened the Universe for me. And, you know, matricide and patricide have always been viewed as among the most horrible, if not *the* most horrible, of all crimes.

Even if we consider God as the Divine Father, the First Law holds. We can't conceivably do physical harm to God, but, presumably, if we sin, we cause Him the Divine equivalent of pain and sorrow, so we must be careful not to do that.

The Second Law would read: *A child must obey the orders given him by his parents, unless that would violate the First Law.*

That's obvious. In modern lax and permissive times, we forget, but parents always *expect* to be obeyed, and in more rigid times—in the days of the Romans or Victorians—they went all apoplectic and psychotic if they were not. Roman fathers had the power of life and death over their children, and I imagine death for disobedience was not completely unheard of. And we all know that God reserves places in Hell for disobedient sinners.

The Third Law would read: *A child must protect its own existence, unless that would violate the First or Second Laws.*

To us, it is rather unthinkable that a parent would expect a child to die or even to suffer injury in the protection of his parents or his obedience to them (thus refraining from violating First and Second Laws). Rather, parents are likely to risk their own lives for their children.

But consider the Divine Father. In the more rigid God-centered religions, such as Judaism, Christianity, and Islam, it is expected that human beings will readily, and even joyously, suffer harm all the way to death by torture rather than transgress the least of God's commandments. Jews, Christians, and Moslems have all gone to their death sturdily rather than do such apparently harmless things as eat bacon, throw a pinch of incense on an idolatrous altar, acknowledge the wrong person as Caliph, and so on. There, one must admit, the Third Law holds.

If, then, we wish to know how robots would react to the loss of human beings, we must see how human beings react to the loss of all-wise, all-powerful parents. Human beings have to find substitutes that supply the loss, and, therefore, so must robots. This is really an obvious thought and is rarely put forward only because most people are very nervous about seeming to be blasphemous. However, back in 1770, that magnificent iconoclast, Voltaire, said, "If God did not exist, it would be necessary to invent him." And if I may be permitted to paddle my rowboat in the wake of Voltaire's ocean liner, I make bold to agree with him.

It follows, then, that if robots are stranded in a society which contains no human beings, they will do their best to manufacture some. Naturally, there may be no consensus as to what a human being looks like, what its abilities are, and how intelligent it might be. We would expect, then, that all sorts of paths would be taken, all sorts of experiments would be conducted.

After all, think how many gods—and with what variety of nature, appearance and ability—have been invented by human beings who had never seen one, but wanted one desperately just the same. With all that in mind, read the fourth entry in the "Robots and Aliens" series.

CHAPTER 1

NEW BEGINNINGS

"So, have you decided on a new name yet?"

"Yes."

Derec waited expectantly for a moment, then looked around in exasperation from the newfound robot to his companions. Ariel and Dr. Avery were both grinning. Wolruf, a golden-furred alien of vaguely doglike shape, was also grinning in her own toothy way. Beside Wolruf stood two more robots, named Adam and Eve. Neither of them seemed amused.

The entire party stood in the jumbled remains of the City Computer Center. It was a testament to Dr. Avery's engineering skills that the computer still functioned at all, but despite the thick layer of dust over everything and the more recent damage from the struggle to subdue the renegade robot that now stood obediently before them, it still hummed with quiet efficiency as it carried out Avery's orders to reconstruct the city the robot had been in the process of dismantling.

The robot had originally called itself the Watchful Eye, but Derec had tired of that mouthful almost immediately and had ordered it to come up with something better. Evidently the robot had obeyed, but. . . .

"Ask a simple question," Derec muttered, shaking his head, but before he could ask a more specific one, such as what the new name might *be*, the robot spoke again.

"I have chosen the name of a famous historical figure. You may have heard of him. Lucius, the first creative robot in Robot City, who constructed the work of art known as 'Circuit Breaker.'"

"Lucius?" Derec asked, surprised. He had heard of Lucius, of course, had in fact solved the mystery of Lucius's murder, but a greater gulf than that which existed between the historical figure and this robot was hard to imagine. Lucius had been an artist, attempting to bring beauty to an otherwise sterile city, while this robot had created nothing but trouble.

"That is correct. However, to avoid confusion I have named myself 'Lucius II.' That is 'two' as in the numeral, not 'too' as in 'also.'"

"Just what we need," Dr. Avery growled. "Another Lucius." Avery disliked anything that disrupted his carefully crafted plan for Robot City, and Lucius's creativity had disrupted it plenty. In retaliation, Avery had removed the creative impulse from all of the city's robots. He looked at his new Lucius, this Lucius II, as if he would like to remove more than that from it.

The robot met his eyes briefly, its expression inscrutable, then turned to the two other robots in the group surrounding it.

"We should use speech when in the presence of humans," Adam said after a moment, and Derec realized that Lucius II had been speaking via comlink.

"Is this your judgment or an order given to you by humans?" asked Lucius II.

"Judgment," replied Adam.

"Does it matter?" Ariel asked.

"Yes. If it had been an order, I would have given it higher priority, though not as high as if it had been an order given directly to me. In that case it would become a Second Law obligation."

The Second Law of Robotics stated that a robot must obey the orders of human beings unless those orders conflicted with the First Law, which stated that a robot could not harm a human or through inaction allow a human to come to harm. Those, plus the Third Law, which stated that a robot must act to preserve its own existence as long as such protection did not conflict with the first two Laws, were built into the very structure of the hardware that made up the robot's brain. They could not disobey them without risking complete mental freeze-up.

Derec breathed a soft sigh of relief at hearing Lucius II refer to the Second Law. It was evidence that he intended to obey it, and, by implication, the other two as well. Despite his apparent obedience since they had stopped him, Derec hadn't been so sure.

Lucius II was still his own robot, all the same. Ariel's question had been an implicit Second-Law order to answer, and he had done so, but now that he had fulfilled that obligation, Lucius II again turned to Adam and Eve and said, "We seem to have much in common." As he spoke, his features began to change, flowing into an approximation of theirs.

Adam, Eve, and Lucius II were not ordinary robots. Where ordinary robots were constructed of rigid metal and plastics, these three were made of tiny cells, much like the cells that make up a human body. The robot cells were made of metal and plastic, certainly, but that was an advantage rather than a limitation, since the robot cells were much more durable than organic cells and could link together in any pattern the central brain chose for them. The result was that the robots could take on any shape they wished, could change their features—or even their gross anatomy—at will.

The other robots in Robot City, with one exception, were also made of cells, but Dr. Avery's programming restricted them to conservative robot forms. Not so with these three. They were not of Avery's manufacture, and without his restriction they used their cellular nature far more than the City robots, forgoing hard angles, joints and plates in favor of smooth curves and smooth, continuous motion. They looked more like metal-coated people than like the stiff-jointed caricatures of men that were normal robots, but even those features weren't constant. They imprinted on whomever was foremost in their consciousness at the time, becoming walking reflections of Derec or Ariel or Avery, or even the alien Wolruf.

At the moment, Adam mimicked Derec's features and Eve mimicked Ariel's. Lucius II, his imprinting programming struggling for control in unfamiliar company, was a more generic blend of features.

Derec found it unnerving to watch the robot's face shift uncertainly between a copy of a copy of his own and of Ariel's. He decided to get the thing to focus its attention on him, and said, "One thing you all have in common is that you're all a lot of trouble. Lucius—Lucius *II*," he added, emphasizing the "II" as if making a great distinction between the former robot and his namesake, "—did you give any thought to what you were destroying when you started this—this *project* of yours?"

"I did."

"Didn't you *care*?"

"I do not believe I did, at least not in the sense you seem to give the word. However, you may be surprised to know that my motive was to restore the city to normal operations.''

"By destroying it?" Avery demanded.

"By rebuilding it. The city was not functioning normally when I awakened here. It was designed to serve humans, but until you arrived, there were no humans. Therefore, I set out to create them. In the process, I found that the city required modification. I was engaged in making those modifications when you stopped me.''

"What you made was a long way from human," Ariel said.

Lucius II had nearly adjusted his features to match Derec's; now they began to shift toward Ariel's again. "You saw only the homunculi," he said. "They were simple mechanical tests run to determine whether complete social functions could be programmed into the later, fully protoplasmic humans. Unfortunately, they proved too limited to answer the question, but the human-making project has enjoyed better success.''

In the voice of someone who wasn't sure she wanted to know, Ariel asked, "What do you mean? What have you done?''

By way of answer, the robot turned toward the computer terminal at Avery's side. He didn't need the keyboard, but sent his commands directly via comlink. By the time everyone else realized what he was doing, he had an inside view of a large, warehouselike building on the monitor. The building was missing a corner, torn completely away in the destruction of only a few minutes earlier, but they could still see what Lucius had intended to show them.

The floor was acrawl with small, furry, ratlike creatures. Lucius II said, "Whereas the homunculi you saw and dissected were completely robotic, and were, as you said, 'a long way from human,' these are actual living animals. In fact, they each carry in their cells the entire genetic code for a human being—all twenty-three chromosome pairs—

but certain genes for intelligence and physical appearance have been modified for the test run. Once I am convinced that the process has no hidden flaws, I will use the unmodified genes to create humans for the city to serve."

"You will do no such thing!" Dr. Avery demanded. "That is an order. When I want humans here, I will put them here myself."

"I will comply with your order. However, you should know that there was no indication of your wishes in the central computer's programming."

"There will be," Avery promised. Derec suppressed a grin. No matter how much he denied it, his father's city was still in the experimental stages as well. He and Derec had both had to make many modifications in its programming to keep it developing properly. True, the complications Lucius II had brought about were not Avery's doing, but the city robots' underlying desire to find and serve humans—and thus, in a sense, Lucius's project—was.

Ariel was staring, horrified, at the creature on the screen as it picked up a scrap of something between its teeth and scuttled out the hole in the wall and out of sight. "That's *human*?" she whispered.

"Not at all," Lucius II said. "It merely uses altered human genes."

"That's—that's *awful*. It *was* human, but you twisted it into something else."

"It was never anything other than what it is."

"It could have been!"

"Certainly. The raw materials making up this city could also have been used to produce more humans. So could a large percentage of the atmosphere. However, the depleted resources that would result from such a usage would not support those humans in any degree of comfort. I made a logical deduction that no thinking being would wish for every combination of chemicals that could possibly become human to actually do so. Was I in error?"

"Yes!" Ariel stared at him a moment, slowly realizing the true meaning of what she'd said, and went on, "I mean, no, you weren't in error in that particular conclusion, but to apply it to already-formed genes is different."

"The genes existed only as information patterns in a medical file until I synthesized them."

"I don't care! They were still—"

"Hold it," interrupted Derec. "This is neither the time nor the place for a philosophical discussion of what makes a human. We can do that just as well at home, where we're more comfortable." Of his father, he asked, "Have you finished your reprogramming?"

"For the time being," Avery replied. "There's more yet to be done, but there's no sense fiddling with the details until the major features are restored."

"Then let's go home. Come on." Derec led the way out of the computer center, through the jumble of wreckage in the corridors—wreckage that robot crews were already at work cleaning up and repairing—and out into the street.

The destruction outside was less evident than what they had seen in the computer center. Entire buildings were missing, to be sure, but in a city that had changed its shape as often as Adam or Eve changed their features, that was no indication of damage. Only the pieces of buildings lying in the street revealed that anything was amiss, and even as they watched, those pieces whose individual cells were still functional began to melt into the surface, rejoining with the city to become part of its general building reserve once again. A few fragments were too damaged to rejoin, but robots were already at work cleaning those up as well, loading them into trucks and hauling them back to the recycling plant.

Avery smiled at the sight, and Derec knew just what was

going through his mind. Transmogrifying robots meant nothing to him; entire cities were his palette.

A row of transport booths waited at the curb just outside the computer center's doorway. The booths were just big enough for one passenger each, little more than meter-wide transparent cylinders to stand in while the magnetic levitation motors in the base whisked their passengers to their destinations. They were a new design, completely enclosed and free-roaming rather than open to the air and following tracks like the booths Derec was used to. Either the destruction had been too great to allow using the track system immediately, and these booths were a temporary measure until the old system was restored, or the City had taken advantage of the opportunity to change the design and this was to be the style from now on. It didn't matter to Derec either way. The booths were transportation, whatever their shape.

Derec boarded one, felt it bob slightly under his weight, and grasped the handhold set into the console at waist level. "Home," he said to the speaker grille beside the handle, trusting the central computer to recognize his voice and check his current address.

Through his internal link with the city computers, he expanded the order. *Bring the others to the same destination*, he sent, turning around to focus on the other members of the group, who were each boarding booths of their own. He sent the image with his order, thus defining which "others" he was talking about.

It was probably unnecessary in all but Lucius II's case, since everyone else knew where they were going, but it never hurt to be certain.

Acknowledged, came the response.

On a whim, Derec sent, *Patch me into receivers in the other booths in this party*.

Patched in.

He could have listened in without going through the computer, but his internal comlink got harder and harder to control the more links he opened with it. Much easier to keep one link open to the computer and let it make the multiple connection.

Derec heard Ariel echo his first command: "Home." Dr. Avery boarded his booth and stood on the platform in silence. Derec smiled. His father was always testing him. Now he was waiting to see if Derec had had the presence of mind to program all the booths.

Send Dr. Avery to same destination via Compass Tower, emergency speed. Do not accept his override, he sent.

Acknowledged.

The Compass Tower was a tall pyramid a few blocks away from Derec and Ariel's home. Before moving in with Ariel and Derec, Avery had had an office/apartment in the apex of it; perhaps he would think that the literal-minded transportation computer had misunderstood Derec's order and was taking everyone to their *own* homes instead of Derec's. He wouldn't realize Derec had played a trick on him until the transport booth failed to stop there. Nor would he be able to change the booth's destination; Derec's command carried exactly the same weight as would his, so the computer would follow the first order received. It was a subtle warning, one Avery would probably not even perceive, but Derec was fed up with his father's little tests, and lately he had taken to thwarting every one of them he could. Avery would never consciously decide to quit, but subliminally, where the impulse to see his son prove himself originated, perhaps he could be conditioned.

Wolruf stepped aboard her booth, saying in her deep voice, " Follow Derec."

Derec's booth had already started to move, but he could still hear the communications going on behind him.

Adam, via comlink, sent, *8284-490-23*. The apartment's coordinates.

Eve sent, *Follow Adam*. Interesting, Derec thought. Adam would rather give the coordinates than admit to following a human, even though he was compelled to do it. Eve, of course, would follow Adam to the end of the universe.

Lucius II, on the other hand . . .

Lucius II sent, *Manual control*.

Denied, the computer responded.

Why denied?

Human command override. Derec has already programmed your destination.

I may also be human. I wish manual control.

Derec's eyebrows shot up. What was this? He'd just convinced the silly thing it was a robot less than half an hour ago!

A loud voice interrupted. "Hey, where are you going?" It was Avery. "Cancel destination! Stop! Let me—"

Not now!

Cancel link to Avery, Derec sent.

Link cancelled, the computer replied, and Avery's voice cut off in mid-word.

The computer had been simultaneously responding to Derec and continuing its conversation with Lucius. Derec heard—*reason for believing that you are human*.

I was grown, not assembled, Lucius II responded. *I am a thinking being, with wishes and desires of my own. My connection to the city computer is completely voluntary. I perceive my own intellectual potentials independent of my programming.*

Visual scanning shows that you are composed of the same cellular material as Robot City robots, or a variant thereof. You are not human.

Lucius II replied, *A robotic exterior means nothing. Check your memory for Jeff Leong.*

Derec gripped the handhold in his transport booth with enough tension to pull a lesser handle from the wall. Jeff Leong! Did Lucius II really think he was a cyborg like Jeff, a human brain in a robot body? And how had he known of Jeff, anyway? That whole incident was long past; Jeff had his human body back again and was off to college on another planet.

Obviously, Lucius had been digging through the computer, accessing records of the City's past, records that Derec had been painstakingly replacing after Dr. Avery had wiped them in his reprogramming over a year ago. It had been Derec's intention to give the City computer—and the robots who used it—the continuous memory of its past that he couldn't have for himself, but that might not have been such a good idea after all, he thought now. Some memories could be dangerous.

Argument understood, the computer responded. *It is possible that you are human. However, I cannot give you manual control even so. Derec's order takes precedence.*

This time, it did. But if Lucius II began issuing orders of his own, next time it might be Derec whose orders weren't obeyed. That wouldn't do.

Lucius II is not human, Derec sent. *He is a robot of the same nature as Adam and Eve.*

Acknowledged.

Derec's transport booth slowed, banked around a corner, and accelerated again. Behind him the others, minus Dr. Avery, executed the same maneuver.

Cancel link to other booths, Derec sent.

Acknowledged.

Derec cancelled his own link to the computer, then focused his attention on the last booth in the line and sent directly, *Lucius, this is Derec.*

Is there another Lucius, or do you mean me, Lucius II?

I mean you. The original Lucius is—Derec was about to say "dead," but thought better of it. No sense fueling the robot's misconceptions with imprecise language.—*inoperative*, he sent. *That means there isn't much chance for confusion. I will simply call you "Lucius" unless circumstances warrant your full title.*

I have no objection. I was not aware that you had a comlink.

There are lots of things you don't know about me. Or about yourself, I believe.

That is true.

I have information you can use.

What information?

You're wrong in assuming you're human. You are an advanced experimental design of robot, just like Adam and Eve.

How do you know this?

I'm the son of the woman who created you.

Lucius thought about that for a long moment. *Perhaps we are brothers*, he said at last.

Derec laughed. *I'm afraid not.*

Perhaps we should ask our mother.

I wish we could, Derec replied.

Why can't we?

Because I don't know where she is.

What is her name?

I don't know that, either.

What do you know about her?

Very little. I have an induced state of amnesia.

This is unfortunate.

Isn't it, though? Derec thought. In a way, his and Lucius's past—and Adam's and Eve's as well—were very similiar. The robots had been planted on three different worlds with nothing more than their basic programming and inherent abilities. It had been up to them to discover their purpose in life, if life is what you wanted to call robot existence.

Similarly, Derec had awakened in a spaceship's survival pod on an ice asteroid, without even the memory of his own name. "Derec" was the name on his spacesuit, a name he had kept even after finding that it was the name of the suit's manufacturer. Like Lucius, he had found himself with only robots for company and questions for comfort. In the time since, he had discovered a few things about himself, most notably that his father was responsible for his condition—it was to be the ultimate "test" of his son's worthiness—but on the whole he had found out pitifully little about his identity. Even now, with his father cured of his megalomania, he still had more questions than answers.

No wonder Lucius had suspected he might be human. For a time, Derec had wondered if he was a robot. In some cases it was a slippery distinction.

I, too, lack a past, Lucius sent.

Learn to like it, Derec replied.

Avery was waiting for them when they arrived. Derec wondered how he had managed that, then realized that it was his own doing. He had sent him off at high speed. Even the long way can be a shortcut if you go fast enough.

"Very funny," Avery said as Derec stepped from his booth.

Derec grinned. "You needed to loosen up."

"I'll remember that." Avery turned and stalked into the apartment building, determined, Derec was sure, to do nothing of the sort.

Derec waited for the others to climb out of their booths, then followed after Avery. The apartment was on the top floor of what was currently a twenty-floor tower, but the height was subject to change without notice. Derec had considered ordering the City to leave the building alone, but in the end had decided against it. Variety was the spice of life, after all. Why should he care how tall the building was? On days when it was too tall for stairs, he could always use the elevator.

Avery had already done so, but the car was already descending again. When it arrived, Derec and everyone else packed into it, and Derec commanded it to take them to the top.

The apartment filled the entire floor. The elevator opened into a skylit atrium filled with plants, surrounding a fountain that Derec had copied from an ancient design. From either side of the pool a solid stream of water arched upward in a parabola, the two streams carefully balanced to meet in the middle and spray outward in a vertical sheet of water. Derec was about to lead on past it, but Lucius paused when he saw it, then reached out and interrupted the path of one stream of water with a hand. The last of the stream continued upward as if nothing had happened, but when the gap reached the center, the other beam arched over to splash against the top of Lucius's hand, just opposite the other water beam. It was obvious that the two beams followed exactly the same trajectory, and could meet anywhere along their paths.

Lucius removed his hand and the two streams met head-on again, the point of contact slowly climbing back up to the center.

"Interesting," he said.

"I call it 'Negative Feedback,'" Derec replied. Unable to resist a little dig, he added, "It's a useful principle. Think about it."

If Lucius understood his implication, he gave no sign of it. "I will," he promised.

Ariel walked on past them, through a massive simulated-wood double door and into the apartment itself. It was a palace. The living room took up one whole quarter of the floor, its glass walls on two sides affording a view of half the city stretching out to the horizon. From the main entryway, a wide, curving hallway led off into the rest of the apartment, one glass wall facing the atrium and the other studded with doors leading into the library, computer room, bedrooms, video room, dining room, kitchen, game room, fitness room, swimming pool, and on into unused space that remained unused only because no one could think of anything else they wanted to fill it with.

The apartment was big and ostentatious, far more than three humans and an alien needed, but as the only inhabitants of an entire city full of robots they had decided to enjoy it. In this particular instance, there seemed little advantage in moderation.

Another robot waited for them in the apartment: Mandelbrot, Ariel and Derec's personal robot. Mandelbrot was a standard Auroran model, made of levers and gears and servo motors, save where damage to his right arm had been repaired with an arm salvaged from a Robot City robot. That arm could have been any shape Mandelbrot—or his masters—wished, but he had chosen to make it match his other arm as closely as possible.

"You beat us home," Derec said when he saw him. Mandelbrot had been in the Compass Tower, helping direct the city's reconstruction from there.

"I left as soon as my task was finished, reasoning that you would come here soon after," the robot replied.

"Right, as usual," Derec said, patting Mandelbrot's metal shoulder in easy camaraderie. He nodded toward Lucius. "Here's our troublesome renegade, ordered to behave and given a new name to remind him of it. Mandelbrot, meet Lucius."

"Hello, Lucius," Mandelbrot said.

"I am more properly called 'Lucius II,' " Lucius said, "to distinguish me from the artist; however, Derec has pointed out that among those who realize the original Lucius is no longer operative, there is little danger of confusion in calling me simply 'Lucius.' "

"That seems reasonable," Mandelbrot replied.

Ariel had already disappeared into the apartment, as had Dr. Avery, but from the soft, synthesized music coming from the living room, Derec knew where at least one of them had gone. He waved the robots into the living room as well, then went into the small kitchen just next door. It held a small automat that provided light snacks and drinks for anyone who didn't want to walk or send a robot all the way to the main kitchen. Derec dialed a number from memory, and the machine delivered up a glass of dark brown, bubbling synthetic cola, one of his own experimental creations.

"Betelgeuse, anyone?" he asked loudly.

"Yecch!" Ariel said from the living room.

Wolruf padded into the kitchen. "I'll 'ave one," she said, holding out her hand. Derec gave her the one he had already dialed for, then ordered another for himself and a glass of Ariel's favorite, Auroran Ambrosia, for her.

From the library Avery said, "Mandelbrot, get me a mug of coffee."

The robot entered the kitchen behind Wolruf, waited patiently for Derec to finish with the automat, then pushed buttons in the sequence for coffee. Derec shook his head in exasperation. Avery had a whole city full of robots at his command, but he still loved to order Mandelbrot around. No doubt it was because Mandelbrot was Derec's robot, and Ariel's before him. Derec had considered telling Mandelbrot to ignore Avery's picayune orders, but so far he hadn't felt like provoking the conflict that Avery so obviously wanted.

Ariel was already sitting in one of the single-person chairs in the living room, her back to the glassed-in corner looking out over the city. Adam and Eve and Lucius were seated on a couch at an angle beside her, looking like a triple reflection of her. Wolruf followed Derec into the room and took another chair opposite the robots, leaving Derec with the choice of a chair beside Wolruf or one across from Ariel. Or—

Convert Ariel's chair into a loveseat, he sent to the apartment controller, and the malleable Robot City material began flowing into the new shape. The chair's right arm receded from Ariel while more material rose up from the floor to fill in the space.

"What the—oh. You could warn a girl."

"But you're so pretty when you're surprised. Your eyes go wide, and you breathe in deep . . ."

"Beast."

"Thank you." Derec handed her the glass of Ambrosia and sat beside her.

He took a long pull at his Betelgeuse. It felt grand to relax. It seemed he'd been going full tilt since he'd first heard of these strange new robots. But now, with Lucius tracked down and ordered to stop his human-creating project, the problems he had caused were over. Completely. One nice thing about robots; once they accepted an order to do something—or not to do it—they were locked into whatever behavior pattern that entailed.

Which, come to think of it, didn't necessarily mean no more trouble. No amount of orders could cover every eventuality, not even a blanket order like, "Don't cause any more trouble." Not even the Three Laws, built into the very nature of their brains, could keep them from occasionally damaging themselves, or disobeying orders, or even harming a human, however inadvertently. It kept such harm to a minimum, surely, but it didn't prevent it entirely. Nor would anything Derec could do keep these robots from letting their curious nature draw them into unusual situations. They were like cats; only dead ones stayed out of mischief.

"So," Derec said, stretching out and putting an arm around Ariel. "What are we going to do with you three?"

Ariel snuggled into Derec's side. The robots looked to one another, then back to Derec. At last Eve spoke. "You need do nothing. We are perfectly capable of taking care of ourselves."

"And causing all sorts of problems in the process. No, sorry, but I think I want to keep an eye on you from now on."

"As you wish."

Lucius said, "I am happy with that arrangement. I will be glad for the opportunity to observe you as well. You are the first humans I have encountered, and since I have been ordered not to create any more, it seems likely that my time will be most profitably spent in your presence."

Still operating under the decision to use speech rather than comlink when with humans, Adam turned to Lucius and said, "Eve and I have observed them for some time now. We are attempting to use our experience to determine what makes humans act the way they do. We intend to formulate a set of descriptive rules, similar to our own Laws of Robotics, which will describe their actions."

"That was one purpose of my project as well."

"When you get it figured out, let us know, okay?" Derec said facetiously.

"We will."

Lucius fixed his eyes on Adam. "What have you learned about them?"

"We have learned that—"

"Hold it," Ariel interrupted. "New datum for all of you. Humans don't like being discussed by robots as if they weren't in the room. If you're going to compare notes, do it somewhere else."

"Very well." The three robots got up as one and walked silently out of the living room. Derec heard footsteps recede down the hallway, pause, then a door that hadn't been there before closed softly. The robots had evidently ordered the building to make them a conference room at the other end of the apartment from the humans.

"Those robots are spooky," Ariel whispered.

" 'Ur rright about that," Wolruf said.

"If they really are my mother's creations, then I'm not sure I want to meet her," Derec added. "They're so single-minded. Driven. And once they do figure out their 'Laws of Humanics,' I'm not sure if I want to be around for the implementation, either."

"What do you mean? No robot can disobey the Three Laws, not even them. We're safe."

"Famous last words. What if they decide we're not fit to be our own masters? What if they decide—like Adam did with the Kin on the planet where he awoke—that they would make wiser rulers than we could? The First Law would require them to take over, wouldn't it?"

"You sound like an Earther. 'Robots are going to take over the galaxy!' "

Derec grinned sheepishly, but he held his ground. "I know, it's the same old tired argument, but if it was ever going to happen, now's the time. Avery's robot cities were spreading like cancer before we stopped them, and for all I know they could take off and start spreading again. Now *these* robots show up, and one of them has already made itself leader of an intelligent race. It wouldn't take much for them to combine their programming and come up with robots who could reproduce themselves faster than humanity can, and who think humans need supervision."

"Not much, except that they can't do it. The first time a human told them they were hurting its normal development, they'd either have to back off or go into freeze-up with the conflict.''

''That's the theory, anyway,'' said Derec.

''Gloom an' doom!'' Wolruf said with a rumbling laugh. '' 'U think 'u 'ave trouble; what about me? I don' even have *that* defense.''

''You don't sound very worried about it.''

'' 'U live where I come from, 'u'd know why. Robots— even alien ones—would make better rulers than what we've got.''

She had a point, Derec thought. When he had first encountered Wolruf, she had been a slave on an alien ship, using her servitude to pay off a familial debt. He doubted that a robot government would allow that kind of arrangement to continue.

But would they allow creativity? Adventure? Growth? Or would there be only stagnation under the robots' protective rule? Derec spent the rest of the day wondering. They were all just abstract questions at this point, but if his parents' reckless experiments got any farther out of hand, the entire galaxy might have the chance to find out the answers.

CHAPTER 2

THE ROBOTICS LABORATORY

Derec awoke to find himself in a splash of sunlight coming in through the window. So east is that way today, he thought automatically. In a city whose buildings moved about and flowed from shape to shape, orienting himself in the morning was a habit he had quickly gotten into. Directions—and landmarks—were too temporary to rely on from day to day.

He became aware that he was alone in the bed. Ariel's absence from his side wasn't surprising, since she tended to be more of a morning person than he was, but the sounds coming from the Personal were. Someone—presumably her, since Avery and Wolruf had their own Personals—was being quite sick.

He got out of bed and padded to the closed door. "Ariel?" he called out hesitantly.

"Don't come in here!" she shouted. There came a sound of rushing water, not quite loud enough to drown completely the sound of her being sick once again.

Derec stood by the door, feeling helpless and, now that

he was uncovered, cold. He took his robe from its hook by the door, put it on, saw hers still there, and took it down as well.

The Personal was silent now. "Are you okay?" he called.

"I am now. Give me a minute."

Still worried, but unwilling to risk Ariel's wrath by opening the door, Derec crossed to the window to look out at the spires and rooftops of Robot City. It looked completely healed now from Lucius's destruction, healed and full of robots going about their normal duties. Derec could see hundreds of them in the streets, on elevated walkways, in transport booths, in maglev trucks, all moving purposefully once again. From this height—twenty-five stories today, Derec guessed—it was hard to tell that all the activity wasn't the ebb and flow of humanity in a fully populated human city.

Behind him he heard more water running, some soft bumping around, the cabinet opening and closing: all normal Personal noises. Then the door opened and Ariel stepped into the bedroom.

She was unselfconsciously nude. Derec turned away from the window, smiled as he always did to see how beautiful she was by light of day, and held out her robe. She let him help her into it.

"You sure you're all right?" he asked.

"Fine, now," she said. "I just woke up feeling sick. Must have been something I ate."

"Maybe." Derec knew she was probably right, but a remnant of the old worry had crept back to haunt him. She had been sick once, deathly sick, and before she had found treatment for it on Earth, Derec had learned what it was to worry about someone's health. That was before they had become lovers; now his concern for her was even more intense.

There might have been another possibility, now that they

were sharing a bed again, but her disease had ruled that out.

"I feel *fine*," she said with exasperation. "Really. And I don't want you telling the robots about this, or they won't rest until they've had me in for a full-blown exam and proven to themselves that I'm healthy."

She had never liked the attention her illness had forced upon her before, either. Derec nodded. "Okay," he said, giving her a strong hug before going over to the closet and picking out a fresh pair of pants and a simple pullover shirt to wear. He wouldn't tell the robots, but he would keep a close watch on her himself today just to make sure she really was okay.

That intention died within minutes of stepping out from the bedroom into the rest of the apartment.

Avery was waiting for him in the kitchen. "What did you do to them?" he asked in his usual belligerent tone.

"Do to whom?" Derec replied calmly, going to the automat and dialing for breakfast.

"The robots," Avery replied.

"The—oh, *those* robots. Ariel sent them off to their room last night to talk business out of earshot. Theirs is the new door at the end of the hallway. Can't miss it."

"I'm *aware* of that," Avery snarled. "What I'm talking about is that the robots are locked up. Inert. Dead."

"What?" Derec turned from the automat with his breakfast still only half ordered.

"Is your hearing going along with your intelligence? The robots are—"

"Locked up. Inert. Dead. I got that. My statement—" here Derec mimicked the tone of a robot so clearly that Avery rolled his eyes to the ceiling, "—was merely a conversational device intended to indicate extreme surprise. And," he added in his own voice again, "to indicate that

I had nothing to do with it. Which I didn't.''

"So you say. You must have said something to make them lock up. Some contradictory order."

"If I did, I don't know what it was." Derec looked back to the automat, shrugged, and pressed the cancel button. "Come on, let's go see."

He padded down the hallway, still in bare feet, to the robot's new room. They hadn't been interested in creature comforts; it was just big enough for the three robots to stand in without bumping into one another or the walls. It held no windows, no chairs—nothing but the robots.

When Derec and Ariel first arrived in Robot City, the robots gave them a small, one-bedroom apartment to live in. It had seemed miserly in a city built on such a grand scale, but the robots had truly thought they were fulfilling the humans' every need. Similarly, the food had been nutritious but bland until they experimented with the automats to get them to produce flavor. Robots simply had no concept of the difference between sufficiency and satisfaction, and now, as Derec looked into the tiny, windowless closet these particular robots had made for themselves, he realized they were still a long way from making that distinction. Either that or their concept of satisfaction was simply so different from the human norm that Derec didn't recognize it when he saw it.

Avery had certainly been accurate enough in his description of them. All three of them were frozen in place, standing up straight, arms at their sides. None of them betrayed the slightest hint of motion.

Derec tried the obvious. "Adam. Eve. Lucius. Respond." Nothing happened.

Avery smiled his "I told you so" smile.

Derec tried the less obvious. *Adam*, *Eve*, *Lucius*, he sent.

At once his mental interface filled with a hiss of static like that from a poorly tuned hyperwave radio. Behind it

Derec heard a faint whine that might have been a signal, but it might have been just noise. On the off chance that they were still receiving, he sent, *I order you to respond.*

Nothing happened.

He cancelled the link and said aloud, "They do seem to be locked up. I got nothing on the comlink, either. I wonder what happened to them."

"We'll find out." Avery—lacking an internal comlink of his own—stalked out of the robots' cubbyhole, went to the com console in its niche in the library, and keyed it on. Into the receiver he said, "I want a cargo team, big enough to carry three robots, up here immediately." He switched it off before the computer could respond.

Derec had followed him into the library. "What are you going to do with them?" he asked.

"Take them to the lab. I'll find out what happened to them, and what makes them tick as well."

Something about Avery's manner made Derec suspect that he wouldn't be restricting himself to non-invasive examination. "You're going to take them apart?"

"Why not?" Avery asked. "It's the perfect opportunity."

Derec didn't know why he felt so disturbed by that thought; he had taken robots apart before himself. But then, when he had done so he had known how to put them back together again, too. With these, Avery had no assurance he could rebuild them when he was done. That was the difference: Avery was considering permanent deactivation, not just investigation.

"Is that reason enough to do it?" Derec asked. "Just because you have the opportunity? They're thinking beings. You should be trying to fix whatever's wrong with them, not cut them open to satisfy your curiosity."

Avery rolled his eyes. "Spare me the sentiment, would you? They're robots. Human creations. Built to serve. If it amuses me to take one apart—or to order one to take itself apart—then I have every right, legal *or* moral, to do so. These robots are a puzzle, and I want to know more about them. Besides that, they've interfered with my own project. I want to make sure they don't do that again.''

''You don't need to destroy them to do that.''

''Maybe I won't. We'll see.''

Derec was of a mind to argue further, but the arrival of the cargo robots interrupted him. There were six of them in the team, and under Avery's direction they moved silently through the apartment, picked up the inert robots unceremoniously by arms and legs, and carried them out to a waiting truck. Avery followed after them, and Derec, struggling into his shoes, came along behind.

''Do you wish the malfunctioning robots taken to the repair facility?'' the truck's robot driver asked as Derec and Avery climbed into the cab with it.

''No,'' Avery said. ''To my laboratory.''

''To your laboratory,'' the driver replied, and with a soft whine of maglev motors, the truck lifted and began to slide down the street.

The truck used the same magnetic levitation principle that the transport booths used, holding itself up off the street and providing thrust with magnetic fields rather than with wheels. It was an old design, but not that common on most worlds even so because of the need for a special track for the magnetic fields to work against. Trains and busses were all maglev, but trucks, which needed the ability to travel anywhere, were usually not.

Here in Robot City, however, all the streets would support maglev vehicles. Everything was made of the same material. There was no place in the city where a maglev truck couldn't go, and thus no reason for them to have wheels. Derec wondered briefly if there were wheels on *anything* here, but couldn't think of a single instance where one was necessary.

Humanity had finally outgrown them, he realized. Or would, when this and the other robot cities on other worlds were opened up for human occupation.

They had hardly gone a block before Derec noticed a flicker of movement in the recessed doorway of one of the buildings lining the street. He looked more closely and saw that it was one of Lucius's rodent-like creations. He looked for more and wasn't disappointed; they were out in force, scavenging the nearly sterile city for food and no doubt starving in the process. They would be able to glean a little nourishment from the occasional strips of grass and ornamental shrubs between buildings, but given as many creatures as Derec saw in just one block, that food supply wouldn't last out the week. Lucius had evidently bred more of them than that one warehouse-full he had shown them yesterday.

Some of the rodents eyed the truck as it glided past, and Derec felt a momentary chill. When they got hungry enough, would they attack?

"We've got to do something about those," he said to Avery, pointing out the window.

Avery nodded his head in agreement. "The robots can round them up. Make fertilizer out of them for the farm."

If they hadn't already *found* the farm, Derec thought, but he supposed that was unlikely. The farm was a *long* way away, partway around the planet.

He thought about Avery's suggestion for a moment, wondering if killing them all was the right solution. He knew they were the result of an experiment that should never have taken place, that they were neither useful nor natural nor even pleasing in appearance, but he still felt uneasy about such a—final solution.

"Maybe we should take the opportunity to start a balanced ecosystem here," he said.

"Whatever for?" Avery asked, obviously shocked by the very idea.

"Well, Lucius was on the right track, in a way. Eventually there will be people living here, but a planet covered with nothing but people and robots and buildings and a few plants is going to be a pretty dull place. They'll want birds and squirrels and deer and butterflies and—"

"What makes you think there are going to be people living here?"

It was Derec's turn to be surprised. "Well, that's the whole point, isn't it? You didn't design these robots to build city after city just for the heck of it. I know you said you did, but that was back when you—well, you know."

"That was when I was crazy, you mean to say."

Derec blushed. "I forget; you don't mince words. Okay, that was back when you were crazy. But now that you're not any more, you can see that the robots eventually have to stop and serve, don't you?"

"Why?"

"Why? You're kidding. If you didn't build all this for people to live in, then what do you intend to do with it?"

The truck slowed coming into an intersection, and another truck flashed by in front of them. Derec flinched, even though he knew the robot driver was aware of the other traffic in the area via comlink. Avery gave no indication that he had even seen the other truck. "I built it as an experiment," he said. "I wanted to see what sort of society robots would come up with on their own. I also wanted to see if you were strong enough to take over the cities with the chemfets I implanted in your system." When Derec began to speak, he raised his hand to cut him off and said, "I've already apologized for that, and I'll do it again. That idea was the product of an insane mind. I had no right to do it, no matter how interesting the result. But the original idea was valid when I had it, and it's still valid now. The cities exist for the robots. I want them to come up with their own society. I think there are basic rules for behavior among intelligent beings—rules that hold true no matter what their physical type—and I think robots can be used to discover those rules.''

For Avery to reveal anything of his plans to someone else, even to his own son, was a rare occurrence. Especially to his son. Avery had never confided any of his plans to Derec, had in fact used Derec at every turn as if he were just another robot. He had tried to *make* him a robot by injecting him with ''chemfets,'' modified copies of the cells that made up the Robot City robots. Derec had survived the infestation, had even arrived at a truce with the miniature robot city in his own body—that was how he had acquired his comlink—but he had not forgotten what his father had done to him. Forgiven, yes, but not forgotten.

Now suddenly Avery was confiding in him. Derec pondered this new development and its significance for the space of a couple of blocks before he said, ''Well, they do seem to be working on it, but I'm not sure I see how anything you come up with from studying robots in a mutable city like this could apply to anything but more robots in an identical city.''

Avery nodded his head vigorously. ''Oh, but it could. In fact, the city's mutability forces the robots' society to be independent of their environment. That's the beauty of it. Any rules of behavior they come up with *have* to be absolute, because there's no steady frame of reference for them to build upon.''

Derec wasn't convinced, but he said, ''So what are you going to do with these rules once you discover them?''

Avery smiled, another rare occurrence, and said, ''That would have to depend on the rules, now wouldn't it?''

Derec felt a chill run up his spine at those words. Ariel and the robots—and Avery himself—had sworn he was cured, but who could be sure? The human mind was still a poorly understood mechanism at best.

Derec had been to Dr. Avery's laboratory once before, as a prisoner. Now, under better circumstances, he had the opportunity to gaze around him in wonder. Every instrument he could imagine—and some he couldn't—for working on robots was there. Positronic circuit analyzers, logic probes, physical function testers, body fabrication machinery—the equipment went on and on. The laboratory would have been positively cluttered with it if it hadn't been so large, but as it was it was simply well equipped. Derec would have bet it was the most advanced such lab anywhere, save that he and Avery were using it to explore the product of a still more advanced one somewhere else.

The three locked-up robots rested atop examining tables that, at first inspection, would have looked at home in a human hospital. A closer look, however, revealed that the pillows under the robots' heads were not simple pillows but were instead inductive sensor arrays for reading the state of a positronic brain. Arm, leg, and body sheaths served a dual purpose: to restrain the patient if necessary and also to trace command impulses and sensory signals flowing to and from the extremities. Overhead stood scanning equipment that would allow the user to see inside a metal body.

There had been a moment of confusion when the cargo robots unloaded the three inert robots from the truck; without conscious control over their mutable shapes, they had all begun to drift back toward their primordial blank state. They had never been easy to identify, but now what few distinguishing features they had were smoothed out, melted. Even so, when viewed from a distance, one of them still seemed faintly wolflike in shape, and that had to be Adam. The ''Kin,'' the dominant life form on the world where he had first come to awareness, was a wolflike animal, and Adam's first imprinting there had evidently become a permanent part of his cellular memory, however faint.

Likewise, Eve displayed just a hint of Ariel's oval face, widely spaced eyes, and gently curvaceous female form, for it had been Ariel upon whom she had first imprinted.

Lucius, having hatched and imprinted in Robot City, still looked more like a robot than either of the others, and for that reason it was he whom Derec and Avery began examining first. Outward form probably didn't mean that the inside would be anything like a normal robot's, or even a normal Robot City robot's, but there was at least a chance of it, and in any case they could learn more from studying a similar form rather than from something completely different.

The positronic brain, at least, was universal among robots of any manufacture, and despite Derec's fear that this might be the exception that proved the rule, the pillow sensor fit itself around Lucius's head without complaint, the indicator light glowing green when the link with the brain had been established.

That alone told them something. Not all robots kept their brains in their heads; some models kept them inside the more protected chest cavity. Avery had designed his to function as much like humans as they could, which meant putting the brain in their heads so they would develop the same automatic responses concerning it. Injury-avoidance behavior, for instance, might be different in a being who kept its brain in a different part of its anatomy. To find the brains in the heads of these robots meant either that they were such excellent mimics that they could determine where their subject's internal organs belonged, or that their creator was also concerned with the subtle differences the location of the brain might introduce into her robots' behavior.

''Definitely getting mental activity,'' Avery said, nodding toward the display screen upon which marched a series of square-edged waveforms. He tapped a button and a different series replaced the first. "Cognition appears undamaged," he muttered, and switched the display again.

Derec suddenly felt a burst of recognition reach through the veil surrounding his past. There on the screen was the basic pattern common to all robots: the Three Laws graphically represented as pathway potentials within the positronic brain. He had learned that pattern years ago, probably in school, though just when it had been he couldn't remember.

It wasn't a major revelation. Derec had already known he had training in robotics, but nonetheless it was a welcome shot of déjà vu. It was a true memory in a mind mostly devoid of them, and as such it was as precious to Derec as gold.

Avery switched the display again.

"Hello, hello, test, test." With each word spoken, what had been a smooth sine wave erupted into a fit of jagged peaks and troughs: Avery's voice processed through the robot's microphone ears.

Derec let out a sigh. The memory was already fading. To avoid the crushing disappointment that so often came from such a tantalizing glimpse into his past, he focused his attention on what was happening before him. "Looks like he's hearing us," he said. "The signal must not be getting processed."

"Let's see." Avery switched the display again, spoke, "Hello, hello, test, test," again, and again the waveform—a modulated square wave this time—burst into activity.

"It's on the main input line." Avery sounded puzzled. He switched again, spoke again, but this time the display remained a constant flat line.

"Aha! Not getting to the command interpreter. Something's blocking it." Avery switched the display back to the input line.

Step by step he focused the monitor deeper and deeper into the brain's positronic pathways, searching for the block, and finally found it in a combination of potentials from the volition circuitry and the self-awareness logic. Plus, the comlink line was saturated with information. The information transfer rate was so high that no other inputs were being monitored.

"I tried listening on the comlink before, but there was just static," Derec said when they discovered the comlink activity. He tried again and heard the same thing as before. "Still there."

"Static, or information flow too fast to recognize?" Avery asked. He pressed keys on a signal processor beside the brain display, and the same static that Derec had heard over the comlink filled the room. Avery began slowing the signal down, and eventually, after being slowed by a factor of one hundred, the static resolved into the familiar bleeps of binary data transfer.

"Sounds like they're having quite a conversation," Derec said.

"Conversation," Avery said disgustedly. "They're ignoring us. That's aberrant behavior. It's already led them into disobeying orders."

"Not really. They only follow the orders they can hear. If they're really not hearing us, then they're not disobeying anything." Derec glanced over at Eve on the next table, and thus Avery's next move took him completely by surprise. Before he knew what was happening, Avery's backhand sent him sprawling on the floor.

"Talk back to me, will you?" Avery screamed. "I've had enough of your insolence, boy! Maybe a boot up alongside your head will knock some respect into you!" He leaped around the table and drew back his foot to follow through on his threat.

Frost, he's flipped again, Derec thought as he twisted frantically to avoid Avery's kick.

Avery screamed in frustration. "Oh, you're quicker than me, are you? We'll see how long that lasts when I shoot you in the leg!" He snatched up a cutting laser from the rack of tools beside the examining table and fired toward Derec, but his shot went wide. Derec heard a loud crack of superheated metal vaporizing, but he was already scrambling for the relative shelter of Eve's table.

Security Alert, he sent over the comlink. *Avery's laboratory. Help!*

He heard another shot, then Avery's quiet laughter, followed by, "Wow, they're really out of it, aren't they?"

Derec stayed silent, gauging the distance from his hiding place to the closest doorway, one leading into one of the lab's other rooms. He was about to make his leap when he heard the scrape of metal sliding on metal, and the laser skidded to a stop beside him.

"False alarm," Avery said.

Derec eyed the laser. Had Avery been playing with him before, or was this just a decoy to get him out into the sights of another laser now? Avery's first shot *had* gone wide, but was that significant? Could he afford to guess wrong?

Well, Derec could play the decoy game as well as Avery. He pulled off his wristcomp and tossed it to his left, over the laser and beyond. The moment it hit the floor he was up and lunging for the tool rack beside Eve's exam table. It tipped over with a crash, spilling equipment across the floor, but Derec was already rolling to his feet with the laser from the rack before the clatter had even begun to die down.

Avery stood beside Lucius, his hands held out to his sides, an amused expression on his face. "It really was a false alarm," he said. "I wanted to test whether or not they'd respond to a First Law imperative."

"Test," Derec spat. "I'm *tired* of your *tests*! You've

been testing me and using me since the day I was born and I'm sick of it! Do you understand me?''

It was then that the six cargo robots burst into the room. They had already left for their normal duties after carrying the other three into the lab, but they were evidently still the closest robots who could answer Derec's frantic summons for help. The first one through the door surveyed the scene and reacted immediately, picking up a small circuit analyzer from a bench by the door and hurling it with all its might at Derec. Before Derec could even flinch, the analyzer knocked the laser from his hands, and both fell to the floor to die in a fit of sparks and smoke. The other robots rushed past the first and split up, two of them going for Avery while three more came for Derec and pinned his arms to his sides. Within seconds both humans were held immobile in the grip of the robots.

"Let me go," Avery said calmly, but the robots didn't budge.

The robot who had knocked the laser from Derec's hands said, "Not until we understand what has happened here. It was master Derec, was it not, who summoned our help?"·

"That's right," Derec said. "He was shooting at me with a laser."

"Yet you were the one holding the laser when we entered."

"I grabbed it in self-defense."

"Defense? I fail to see how a weapon can be used for defense."

Derec blushed under his father's sudden onslaught of laughter. "He's got you there!" Avery said.

The robot had, Derec realized. If he'd actually used the laser, he would have been guilty of the very action he was defending himself against. In the robot's eyes, harm to a human was harm to a human, no matter what the provocation.

It was embarrassing to have such a thing pointed out to him. He should have realized it from the start, should have felt an instinctive, rather than belated, urge to preserve his attacker as well as himself from harm.

Even if that attacker was his father.

"I stand corrected," he said at last. "I should have retreated."

"I am glad you realize that," the robot said. Of Avery it asked, "Why did you shoot at him?"

"I needed to provoke a First Law response in these robots. I didn't shoot directly at him, just close."

"I see," the robot said, scanning the room for verification. It probably *did* see, Derec realized. The heat trails of his path and the path of the laser beam would still be visible in infrared light; it would be easy for the robot to tell how close the beam had come.

"Do you accept his explanation?" the robot asked Derec.

"I guess," Derec said with a sigh.

"Do either of you wish to continue your hostilities?"

Derec shook his head. "No."

"No," echoed Avery.

"Very well." Derec felt the robots let go of his arms, but the ones holding Avery still held him. The first robot, moving to stand closer to him, said, "You should understand that psychological shock, especially shock concerning fear for one's life, is still considered harm to a human. You have caused Derec harm. Do you understand this?"

Avery scowled. "Yeah," he said. "Let me go."

"Only when I am convinced that you will not repeat your offense. Do I have your assurance that you will not?"

"Okay, okay, I won't shoot at him again."

"You must also endeavor never to scare him in another way, or to harm him either physically or psychologically in any way. Do I have your assurance that you will not?"

"*Yes*, you have my assurance. Now let me go."

The robot turned to Derec. "Do you accept his assurance as truthful?"

Derec couldn't resist laughing. "Hardly," he said. "But that's okay. After what he just did, I don't think he *can* surprise me anymore. Let him go."

The robots did. "We will observe you for a time," the talkative one said.

Avery scowled. "I don't want you to. Go away."

"We cannot do that until we are sure that you will not harm one another."

Avery evidently realized this was an argument that he couldn't win. He shrugged and gestured at the mess on the floor. "Make yourselves useful then."

The other robots began to pick up the scattered equipment, but the talkative one said to Avery, "A less destructive First Law test would have been to simply state that you were about to fall over without catching yourself. No properly functioning robot would allow that to happen."

"Thank you for your profound input," Avery said with exaggerated politeness.

"You are welcome."

"Now get to work."

CHAPTER 3

THE BIOLOGICAL LABORATORY

"I still think we ought to take one of them apart." Avery was leaning over Lucius, positioning the internal scanner for yet another cross-section through the robot's body. It may have resembled a robot on the outside, but that was as far as the similarity went; Lucius's interior resembled a human body far more than it did a robot's. It didn't have any unnecessary internal organs, but those it did need were modeled after the human pattern. It had bunches of cells arranged like muscles, bones, and nerves, at least, rather than the more conventional linkages and cams.

Interesting as that discovery was, it had been hours since they had made it, and Avery was getting frustrated.

"And I still say it won't tell us anything we can't find out indirectly," Derec replied. He was sitting on a stool on the opposite side of the examination table, watching the screen and getting bored. "They're obviously comparing notes, probably on their experience with humans. Why not let them go for a while? They might come up with something interesting.''

"Like some wonderful new way to disturb my cities," said Avery.

"Your cities can take care of themselves. And if not, I can take care of them."

"You think so. I think you're just trying to protect your mother's experiment."

Derec considered that possibility. Was he trying to protect her experiment, or was he simply trying to protect three robots from being needlessly destroyed? He had thought it was the latter, but now that Avery mentioned it . . .

"Maybe I am," he said.

"You don't even know her."

"That's not my fault."

"And it *is* mine. Guilty. I shouldn't have wiped your memory. When I think of a good way to make it up to you, I will, but believe me, you're better off without it."

"I'd like to be the judge of that."

Avery had been looking at the scanner display, but now he turned his head and looked his son straight in the eyes. "Of course you would. I can understand that. But bear in mind, if you got your memory back, what you'd have memories *of*. I told you once before that you had a fairly normal childhood, and that's true enough, but it was a normal childhood in an Auroran family, which is the next best thing to no family at all. Your mother and I hardly saw one another after your birth. You hardly saw either of us. In fact, you spent most of your childhood with robots."

"No wonder I fit in so well here," Derec said drily.

Avery said nothing, and Derec sensed his embarrassment. At least he's embarrassed, he thought, then chided himself for feeling vindictive. Learning to live with a recovering psychopath was almost as difficult as being the recoveree.

The things his father had done while insane were not his fault, at least not in the sense that he could be held responsible for them, yet Derec still felt that he had been poorly treated. *Somebody* should feel bad about it, shouldn't they?

Or was this another situation like the one they had just gone through with the laser? Was wishing for remorse just another way of mistreating a human?

No wonder the robots were having such a time trying to understand human interactions. The humans themselves didn't understand them half the time.

But the robots were learning. Witness the cargo robots, still standing patiently around the lab, watching for signs of recurring violence. They had already learned not to trust a human's stated intentions.

How could that be a good thing? Before long these robots of his father's would decide that humans were not to be trusted at all, and hence not to be obeyed in any situation where trust was necessary to avoid an internal conflict with the Three Laws. As for his mother's robots, if they ever came out of their communication fugue, who could predict what conclusions they would draw from their collective experiences? The only prediction Derec was willing to make with any certainty was that they would be even less useful than before.

That thought made Derec ask, "What were our house robots like?"

Avery looked up momentarily in surprise. "What do you mean, 'what were they like?' Like robots, of course. Old-style robots. I didn't develop the cellular robot until after you'd left home, and your mother stole her design from me."

"That's what I thought. The point is, they did the mundane work for you, right? Cooking and cleaning and changing diapers and emptying the trash."

"Of course they did," Avery said. He sounded indignant, as if the very thought that *he* would have done any of those chores was obscene.

"They were useful, then."

"What are you getting at?"

"I'm getting at the obvious observation that the robots around here, despite their advanced design—maybe *because* of their advanced design—aren't as useful as the older models. They're more trouble. Too much independence."

Avery moved the scanner a fraction and keyed the display again. Another view into the nerve and musclelike masses of Lucius's interior appeared on the screen. "Maybe my definition of useful is different from yours," he said.

They had already had that conversation. Avery was simply not interested in immediate utility, and Derec was. There was no sense arguing over it. Derec got up off his stool with a sigh, stretched, and said, "I'm about to fall asleep here. Are you going to keep at it all day?"

"Probably," Avery replied.

"I think I'll leave you to it, then."

"Fine."

"Just don't cut any of them up, okay?"

Avery looked pained. "I'll do with them whatever I please. If that includes cutting them up, then that's what I'll do."

Derec and Avery stared at one another across the unmoving robot's body for long, silent seconds. One of the cargo robots near the wall took a step toward them. Derec looked up at the robot, then back to Avery. He considered ordering the robot to keep Avery from harming the others, but decided against it. It would just escalate the war between them. Besides, there were better ways.

He shrugged and backed off. "It's your conscience. But I'm asking you, please don't cut any of them up. As a favor to me."

Avery frowned. "I'll think about it," he replied.

Derec nodded. Now it was up to Avery to decide whether or not to escalate the war. It was a risk, but a calculated one. Derec had felt a spark of humanity in Avery a couple of times today; he was willing to bet his father was sick of confrontation, too.

"Thanks." He turned away and said to the cargo robots, "Come on, the rest of you. You can take me back home and then get on with whatever else you were doing."

He really had intended to go home, but on the way there the sight of Lucius's creatures still scavenging in the streets reminded him that he still had to do something about them, and soon, or they were going to start eating each other. With Lucius himself out of commission, there was only one good place to start, and it wasn't at home. "I've changed my mind," he said to the robot driving the truck. "Take me to Lucius's lab instead."

The robot hesitated a long time—nearly the length of a block—then asked, "Which one do you wish to visit?"

"How many has he got?"

"The central computer lists thirty-seven separate laboratories."

"*Thirty-seven?*"

"That is correct."

"What did he do with that many labs?"

The cargo robot was silent for a moment as it conferred with the computer again, then said, "Fifteen were dedicated to fabricating the artificial humans he called 'homunculi' and are now abandoned. The other twenty-two are engaged in fabricating humans."

"*Are* engaged? Still?"

"That is correct."

"We told him not to continue with that!"

"That is also correct."

The cargo robot offered no more explanation, but Derec could see plainly enough what the situation was. Lucius had interpreted his orders to mean only him, leaving the other robots who had been helping him free to continue the project. Well, he would put a stop to that soon enough.

But twenty-two labs! No wonder the city was full of rats.

"Take me to the one he showed us yesterday," Derec said.

The driver evidently had no problem with Derec's inclusive "us," nor with finding the appropriate lab in the computer's records. It slowed the truck and turned left at the next corner, made another left turn at the next block and they went back the way they had come for a while, then turned right and went on for block after block through the city. The rat population on the streets dwindled, then grew larger again as they left the sphere of influence of one lab and entered another. Evidently Lucius had felt no need to cluster his workplaces.

Derec, watching the towering buildings slide past, felt again how empty the city was without people in it. None of these buildings had any real purpose, nor did the robots in them, save for Avery's nebulous experiment in social dynamics. And what could possibly come of that? The robots weren't creating a society of their own; they were instead simply building and rebuilding in anticipation of someday having humans to serve. And some of them, he thought wryly, were busy building those humans. All because of the Three Laws of Robotics and the poorly defined quantity, "human," those Laws directed them to protect and obey.

Derec had felt a great sadness pervading the city since he first arrived. It felt almost haunted to him, the robots wandering about like lost souls, purposeless. He was attributing human qualities to inhuman beings, he knew, but Frost, they didn't have to be human to be lost, or to feel sad about it. Robots were intelligent beings, no matter what their origin, and it behooved their creators to treat them kindly. That included giving them a sense of purpose and letting them fulfill it. It seemed clear to Derec that none of these Robot City robots, nor the ones lying inert in Avery's lab, had been treated well by their creators.

Humans make poor gods, he thought wryly.

The cargo robots dropped Derec off outside a low, non-descript warehouselike building. If it was the same one Lucius had shown them the day before, then it had been repaired, but not before a veritable horde of the rat-creatures had escaped. Two hordes, Derec decided as he watched them scurrying about through the streets. They had been thick in the other parts of town, but this was ridiculous.

He ran from the truck to the main door, sending rats squealing off in all directions, but none chased after him.

Yet, he thought.

Directly inside the main door a hallway led down the length of the building, with doors opening to either side. Derec walked down the hallway, expecting to find a laboratory sufficient in complexity to support a complete genetic engineering project, but when he peered through the first doorway to his right, he couldn't help laughing. Avery was the mad scientist, but Lucius's lab—at least this part of it— was the typical mad scientist's lair. Vats of bubbling brew stood in various stages of incubation or fermentation or whatever was going on along one wall, while electrical devices of various natures hummed and clicked contentedly over them. A bank of cages along another wall held a be-wildering array of small creatures, ranging from insects to something that might have been a mouse to one of the rodentlike creatures now overrunning the city. Another wall held trays of growing plants. In the center of the room, table after table held enough interconnected glassware to distill a lake. From the entire collection came a mixture of smells stronger and more varied than from an explosion in a kitchen automat.

The necessity of dealing with organic material had forced the lab into the configuration he saw, but Derec found it funny nonetheless. The gleaming robots who tended the equipment made it even more so by contrast. They should have been wearing dark robes and walking with stooped posture.

One of them walked past carrying a test tube filled with cloudy liquid. Derec cleared his throat noisily and said, "We've got a problem here."

"That is unfortunate," the robot answered without pausing in its stride. "How may I help?" It walked on over to a centrifuge, put the tube inside, and started it spinning.

Derec felt momentary annoyance at talking to a robot who was too busy to stop for him, but some remnant of his thoughts on the trip over kept him from ordering the robot to drop what it was doing. This robot, at least, had a purpose. A wrong one, but maybe they could do something about that without defeating it completely.

"To start with," he said, "you can't create any humans. That goes for all of you, in all of these labs. Is that clear?"

"Yes," the robot replied. It looked at Derec, then back to the centrifuge. If it was disappointed, it didn't show it.

"All right. Next, then, I need to know what those creatures—" Derec waited until the robot looked to see where he was pointing, "—there at the end of the line—eat."

"They are omnivorous," the robot replied, gathering up a handful of empty tubes from a box and inserting them one by one into some sort of diagnostic instrument beside the centrifuge.

"There's a whole bunch of them running loose in the city without a food supply. We need to give them one."

"That would only increase their numbers. Is that what you wish to do?"

"No. But I don't want them to starve, either."

"We have discovered that if they do not starve, they will reproduce. There is no intermediate state. The number of creatures existing now are the result of a large food supply, which we have ceased providing."

"You intend for them to starve, then?" Derec watched the robot push buttons on the face of the instrument.

"That is correct."

"Why not introduce something that eats *them*?"

"That seems needlessly complex. Starvation will reduce their numbers equally well."

"I see." Derec felt somehow vindicated to hear the robot's answer. Evidently robots didn't make very good gods, either.

He thought of Avery's suggestion to have the robots collect and kill them. A typical Avery idea, little better than the robots' starvation plan. Much as he wanted to avoid conflict, Derec couldn't let that happen, either.

"Look," he said, going on into the lab and pulling up a stool, "even if you can't make humans, this project of yours can still be good for something. Let me tell you about balanced ecosystems. . . ."

The sun was long down by the time he made it home that night. Ariel was in the library, leaning back on a couch with her feet up on a stool and listening to one of Avery's recordings of Earther music while she read a book. Neither Avery nor Wolruf were in evidence, though the loud snoring coming from down the hallway was suggestive of at least one of them. Mandelbrot stood in a wall niche behind Ariel, waiting for her to need his services.

Ariel put down the book and scowled at Derec in mock hostility when he entered the room. "Forget where you lived?" she asked.

"Almost." Derec sat down beside her on the couch and

nuzzled her neck playfully. "I've been trying to plan a simple ecosystem for the city, but it's a lot tougher than I thought. Do you realize that you have to balance everything right down to the microbes in the soil? Pick the wrong ones, or not enough varieties of the right ones, and your whole biosphere goes crazy."

"Is that so?"

"Yes, that's so. I've been studying it all day."

"Sounds exciting." She yawned wide, and the book slipped from her fingers to land with a thump on the floor. "Oops. Tired."

Derec scooped it up for her and laid it on the couch's armrest. "It's late. We should go to bed."

"I guess we should."

Derec took her hand and helped her up from the couch. She let him lead her into the bedroom, where he pulled down the covers and left her on the foot of the bed to undress and crawl in while he used the Personal.

When he came out, she was already asleep. He slid quietly into bed beside her and within minutes he was out as well, dreaming of food chains and energy flow.

But once again, he awoke to the sound of someone throwing up in the Personal. He sat up with a start, his heart suddenly pounding. The sun barely reached the window this time, but it was up. It was morning, and Ariel was sick.

His heart was still pounding when she opened the door and looked out at him. "Does this mean what I think it means?" he asked.

"I don't know," she said. "But I think we'd better find out."

The urine test came up positive, as they knew it would. Even so, it was hard for either of them to remain standing when the medical robot said, "May I be the first to offer you congratulations on the occasion of—"

"Wow," Derec murmured. He and Ariel had been holding hands in anticipation; now he squeezed hers tightly.

"Oh," Ariel said, her hand suddenly going slack. "I don't—"

"But how?"

"I wasn't supposed to be able to—"

"The cure!" Derec wrapped his arms around her and picked her up off the ground in a hug. "When they cured your amnemonic plague on Earth, they must have 'cured' your birth control, too."

"They might have warned me."

Derec's grin faltered. He set her back on her feet again. "What's the matter? Don't you want—?"

Ariel took the two steps necessary to reach a chair and sat heavily. "I don't know," she said. "It's just such a shock. I'm not ready for it."

"Well, we've got plenty of time to get used to the idea. At least, I think we do." Derec turned to the medical robot. "How far along is she?"

"Fifteen days, plus or minus a day," answered the robot. "A blood test would be more accurate, but I discourage invasive testing for such minor gain."

"Me too," Ariel said. She held out her hand and Derec took it again. "Well. Two weeks. That leaves us a while yet." She looked down the corridor into the empty expanse of the hospital, then back to Derec.

Derec squeezed her hand again for reassurance. He wouldn't say he knew just how she felt, because he wasn't the one whose body would swell with the developing baby, and he wasn't the one who would have to go through the painful process of giving birth, but he did at least share the sudden confusion of learning that he was going to be a parent. Did he want to be a father? He didn't know. It was too soon to be asking that sort of question, and at the same time, far, far too late. He was going to be one whether he wanted to be or not.

Well, it wasn't like he couldn't provide for a child. He had an entire city at his disposal, and more scattered throughout the galaxy, all full of robots who were hungry for the chance to serve a human. He certainly didn't have to worry about food or housing or education. Childhood companions might be a problem, though, unless they could bring some more families to Robot City. Derec wondered if Avery would stand for it. If not, then Derec could build his own city. It wouldn't take much; a few seed robots and a few weeks' time. Or there was still their house on Aurora, come to think of it. Derec and Ariel had both grown up on Aurora; perhaps their child should as well.

All those thoughts and more rushed through Derec's mind as he held Ariel's hand in the hospital waiting room. He grinned when he realized how quickly he had begun planning for the baby's future. It was an instinctive response; hormones that had been around since before humanity learned to use fire were directing his thoughts now. Well, he didn't mind having a little help form his instincts. In this situation, it was about all he had to go on.

Looking at Ariel, he felt a sudden rush of warmth course through him. He wanted to protect her, provide for her, help her while she bore their child. Was that instinct, too? He had been in love with her before, but this was something else.

He certainly hadn't learned it on Aurora. His father had been right: an Auroran family was the next thing to none. Permanent attachments, or even long-term relationships, were rare, even discouraged. An attachment as deep as he felt now for Ariel would be considered an aberration there.

Which meant that it wasn't instinct, or Aurorans would have been feeling it, too. Somehow that made Derec feel even better. It was genuine love he was feeling, concern and care born of their experiences together, rather than simple chemicals in his bloodstream. Instinct was just intensifying what he already felt for her.

She was worried. He could feel it in her hand, see it on her face. She needed time to accept what was happening to her. On sudden impulse, he said, "Let's go for a walk."

She thought about it for a few seconds. "Okay."

He helped her to her feet. The medical robot said, "Before you go, I need to impress upon you the importance of regular medical checkups. You should report for testing at regular two-week intervals, and before that if you notice any sudden developments. Your health is critical to the developing embryo, and its health is critical to your own. Also, your diet—"

Ariel cut him off. "Can this wait?"

"For a short time, yes."

"Then tell me later. Or send it to our apartment and I'll read up on it there."

The robot hesitated, its First Law obligation to protect Ariel and her baby from harm warring against its Second Law obligation to obey her order. Evidently Ariel's implied agreement to follow its instructions was enough to satisfy its First Law concern, for it nodded its head and said, "Very well. But do not overexert yourself on your walk."

Derec led her out of the hospital and along the walkway beside the building, ignoring the row of transport booths waiting by the entrance. They walked in silence for a time, lost in their own thoughts, taking comfort from each other's presence, but within a few blocks they had a silent host of Lucius's rodents following them, their hungry stares and soft chittering noises sending shivers up Derec's spine. He didn't know how dangerous they might be, but if nothing else, they were certainly spoiling the mood. With a sigh, he led Ariel back inside another building and up the elevator to the top, where they continued their walk along enclosed paths high above the streets. The rats hadn't yet reached these levels.

The tops of some of the buildings had been planted with grass and trees to make pocket parks; after passing three or four of them—all devoid of activity save for their robot gardeners unobtrusively tending the plants—they stopped to sit in the grass beneath a young apple tree and look out over the city. Ariel had been quiet for a long time now, but Derec couldn't take the silence anymore. He felt an incredible urge to babble.

"I'm still not sure I believe it's really happening," he said. "It's crazy to think about. A new person. A completely new mind, with a new viewpoint, new thoughts, new attitudes, new everything. And we're responsible for its development. It's daunting."

Ariel nodded, "I know what you mean. Who are we to be having a baby?"

"Better us than Lucius, at least," Derec said with a grin.

"I suppose. At least we know what one *is*." Ariel tried to smile, but hers was a fleeting smile at best. She turned away, said to the city, "Oh, Derec, I don't know. I don't know if I want to do this. I keep thinking about having it, and then I keep thinking about not having it, and right now I've got to say that not having it sounds a lot better to me." She looked back to Derec, and he could see the confusion written plain as words in her expression.

His own face must have mirrored her confusion. "Not having it," he said. "You mean . . . you mean . . . aborting it?" The instincts, or hormones, or whatever they were, still had a strong grip on him. It was hard to even say the word that would take his child from him.

"Yes, that's what I mean," said Ariel. "Aborting it. Stopping it now, while we still can. It's not like we wanted it, is it? We weren't trying for one. We were happy without it. If we'd known I *could* get pregnant, then we would have been using birth control, wouldn't we? So why should we change our entire lives because of some silly—accident?"

"Because it's *us*! *Our* child. *Because* it's a new person, a new mind, with a new viewpoint and all that. That's why we should keep it." Was that why? Derec fought for his own understanding even as he tried to explain it to Ariel. "It's—do you remember what it was like when we first found ourselves here? Me without a memory at all, yours slowly slipping from you, neither of us with any idea what we were doing here? Remember how lost we felt?"

Ariel's eyebrows wrinkled in concentration. "It's fuzzy that far back. But I know what you're talking about. I've felt lost often enough since then."

"Right. We had no purpose; that's why we felt that way. I spent my time trying to track down my father, thinking he could help restore my memory, but that was just a yearning for the past. We spent time searching for a cure for your disease, but that was just patching up the past, too. Now I find I've got a mother running around out here somewhere, too, and I was all set to spend however long it takes trying to find her, to see if she couldn't do for me what Avery won't, but now I don't even care. Now all of a sudden we have something to look forward to, something in our future. Who cares about the past when we've got that?"

Ariel shook her head. "Why should we grab at the first thing that comes along? Derec, this is going to change our *lives*. Unless we want to put the baby in a nursery, and it's obvious you don't, then we're going to have to take care of it. We're going to have to *live* with it, like Earthers and settlers do. Do you really want that? I'm not so sure I do. And besides that—" she waved away his protest, "—it's my body we're talking about here. Pregnancy is dangerous. It can cause all sorts of problems in a woman; blood clots, kidney damage—you wouldn't believe all the things that can go wrong. And for what? A future with a squalling brat in it? I can't see risking my life for that.''

"But what about the baby's life? Isn't that a consideration?''

"Of course, it's a consideration," Ariel said angrily. "If it wasn't, I'd have had the medical robot abort it this morning. I'm still trying to weigh it out; my life and my future versus the life and future of what at this point amounts to a few dividing cells. It's a testament to how important I think it is that I'm considering it at all.''

Derec had been subliminally aware of the gardener going about its job somewhere behind him. The soft whirr of the robot's grass-cutting blade had been a soothing noise at the edge of his perception, but the sudden silence when it stopped was enough to make him look around to the robot, just in time to see it topple onto its side, smashing a bed of flowers when it hit.

"What the—?" He stood, went over to the robot, and said, "Gardener. Do you hear me?''

No response.

Gardener, he sent via comlink.

Still nothing. He pulled it up to a sitting position, but it was like raising a statue. The robot was completely locked up. Derec let it fall on its side again. It made a quiet thud when it hit the ground.

"It couldn't handle the conflict," Derec said in wonder. "Its First Law obligation to protect you was fighting with its obligation to protect the baby, and it couldn't handle it.''

"You sound surprised," said Ariel. "I'm not. It's tearing me apart, too.''

Derec left the robot and went back to Ariel, sitting beside her and wrapping her in his arms.

"I wish it wasn't.''

"Me too.''

"What can I do to help?''

Ariel shook her head. "I don't know. Yes, I do. Just don't push me, okay? I know you want to keep it, but I've got to decide on my own whether or not I do. Once I know that, we can talk about what we're actually going to do. Okay?"

"Okay."

As if to confirm her independence, Ariel pulled away and closed her eyes in thought. Derec leaned back in the grass and looked up through a tangle of leaves at the sky. An occasional cloud dotted the blue.

Did every new parent go through this? he wondered. Could what he and Ariel were feeling be normal? Did Avery and his mother agonize over whether or not to have him? He couldn't imagine Avery agonizing over any decision. His mother must have, though. She must have wondered if Derec would be worth the effort of childbirth. Evidently she had decided so, probably *before* she became pregnant, come to think of it, since she'd had no reason to believe she was infertile as Ariel had.

She and Avery must have been in love then. What a concept; someone loving Avery. Or was she just like him? Had their decision to have a child been nothing more than the practical way to acquire someone to experiment on?

It didn't matter. He and Ariel were in love; that was what mattered. The thought of staying with Ariel until their child grew up didn't scare him. Derec knew that parents on most planets didn't worry about that kind of responsibility—even parents more fond of one another than his own—but he intended to. The thought of raising a child gave his life direction, gave him a sense of purpose he hadn't even realized until now he was missing.

Ariel, evidently realizing he wouldn't pressure her whether he held onto her or not, lay down in the grass beside him, resting her head on his chest. His arms went around her automatically, and it felt perfectly natural to be holding her so. It felt right. For a time, as they watched the clouds drift past overhead, the rooftop garden seemed to become their whole universe, and it was a good universe.

Ariel's thoughts had evidently been paralleling his own, but along a different track. "I'm glad we're not on Earth any more," she said suddenly. "I'd feel even worse there."

"No kidding." Derec shuddered. With a population in the billions, Earth was no place to be having children. There, where the population density in the enclosed cities could be measured easily in people per square meter, every new mouth to feed was a tragedy, not a blessing.

And what was worse, too few of the people there were worried enough to do anything about it. Here stood an entire planet covered with city, full of robots eager to share it, yet Derec doubted if he could find enough people in all of Earth to fill even the section he could survey from this one rooftop. Most of them hated space, hated robots, and on an even more fundamental level, hated change. They wouldn't leave Earth even for a better world.

A few of them would. After a long hiatus, Earth had once again begun settling alien worlds, but the fraction of its population involved was insignificant. The birth rate there would replace its emigrants before they could achieve orbit.

It was a sobering thought. Derec recalled Lucius's words to Ariel at their first meeting, his assertion that no thinking being would want every human who might possibly exist to do so, but it seemed as if Earthers were doing their best to ensure just that. They seemed intent on turning their entire biosphere into a teeming mass of humanity.

An irrational fear washed over him, the fear that Earth society would somehow intrude upon his happiness even here, that its riot of bodies could somehow threaten even Robot City. Derec felt his heart begin beating faster, his breathing tighten, as he considered his child's potential enemies.

Hormones! he thought wryly a second later. Paranoia was evidently a survival trait.

"To space with Earth," he said, tickling Ariel playfully in the ribs. "We're beyond all that."

The sun had shifted position considerably when Derec awoke. He couldn't tell whether it was from the simple passage of time, or if the building had moved beneath them while they slept. Probably both, he decided. He lay in the grass, Ariel still sleeping with her head on his shoulder, while he decided whether or not to get up.

A noise from beyond the edge of the building made the decision for him. Someone had screamed! Derec was up in an instant, leaping for the railing around the edge and peering down.

A hunter-seeker robot—a stealthy, black-surfaced special-function 'bot with advanced detection circuitry—stood in the center of an intersection, pivoting slowly around in a circle. A rustle of motion in a doorway caught its attention and it stopped. It raised its right hand, pointing with the forefinger extended, and a bright red laser beam shot out from its finger toward the doorway. Another scream echoed off the buildings.

Derec looked up the street. Every intersection, for as far as he could see, had a hunter-seeker standing in it. Avery had ordered them to clean up the rodents—his way.

Stop! he sent to them. *Cease hunting activity.*

The hunter closest to him looked upward, and Derec felt a momentary urge to back away from the railing. Any robot—and Derec as well, for that matter—could tell what general direction a comlink signal was coming from, but a hunter-seeker could pinpoint the source—and shoot at it. But the robot couldn't fire at him. It would see instantly who he was, and the First Law would prevent it. Derec stayed at the railing and sent, *You are ordered to cease killing those creatures.*

I am sorry, master Derec. I already have orders to kill them.

"What's going on?" Ariel asked sleepily from his side. She leaned against the railing and looked down.

"Avery's ordered the robots to kill all of Lucius's rodents. I'm trying to get them to stop." *I order you not to kill them,* he sent. *You should respect life.*

I respect human life. That is all.

Those creatures carry human genes.

That has been explained to me. That does not make them human. As the hunter spoke, another rodent made a dash for safety, but the hunter twitched its hand in a blur of motion, the beam shot out, and the rodent tumbled end over end in the street, screaming. The hunter fired again and the screaming stopped.

They certainly have human vocal apparatus, Derec thought.

Damn it, you're upsetting me. Stop it!

The hunter robot paused at that, but evidently Avery had warned it to expect such a ploy. *I regret that I cannot,* it said. *Your displeasure is not as important as your safety. These creatures could pose a safety hazard.*

You don't know that.

I have been ordered to consider them as such. The hunter turned its attention back to the street. It resumed its search, shooting again at another rodent. This time the rodent died silently, and Derec realized that the robot was attempting to limit his discomfort by making a clean kill.

Derec tried to think of a way to get around Avery's programming, but no solution came to mind. Avery had made his orders first and stressed that they were to be followed no matter what Derec said; there was very little Derec could do to counter them now.

How fickle a robot's behavior could be under the three laws! A robot gardener could lock up at the mere mention of a life-threatening dilemma involving humans, but the hunter-seekers could shoot rodents all day long. None of them cared about life in general. Not even the gardener truly cared about his charges except for their potential to please a human.

How could that be right? Even the cruelest human cared about something. Derec was willing to bet even Avery had a soft spot for kittens or puppies or *something*. How could he ever expect a society of robots to mimic a human society if they held no reverence for life?

"Come on," Derec said, seething with righteous indignation. "Let's go home."

His anger had mellowed a bit by the time they reached their apartment, but it flared to life again the moment he saw Avery standing by the living room window, watching his hunter-seekers at work. He was about to start a shouting match, but Mandelbrot's sudden exclamation switched the topic of discussion before he ever had a chance.

"Congratulations, Ariel!" said the robot the moment he saw them enter the apartment.

"Shh!" she told him, forefinger to her lips, but the damage had been done.

Avery turned away from the window. "Congratulations? Whatever for, Mandelbrot?"

His question was a stronger order to speak than Ariel's whispered command to be quiet. The robot said, "Mistress Ariel is preg—"

"Shut *up*!"

Mandelbrot stiffened, the conflict of orders creating a momentary Second Law crisis.

"Preg," Avery said into the silence. "Preg*nant* perhaps? Are you, my dear?" His voice was all honey, but neither she nor Derec was fooled. Avery had opposed their association from the start, was instrumental in separating them when they had first become lovers on Aurora, and had done everything he could to keep them from redeveloping an affection for one another when circumstances had forced them back into close company. He was less than happy at the news, and they knew it.

"Don't strain yourself smiling," Derec growled.

Avery shook his head. "You sound overjoyed. One would suppose you weren't ready for it. Is that it? Did it take you by surprise?"

"None of your business," Ariel said.

"Of course not. However, as a father myself, I do have a certain interest in the situation. You may be happy to know that it is reversible."

Ariel shot him a dark look. "I'm aware of that." She turned away, heading down the hallway toward her and Derec's room.

"Good," Avery said to her receding back. He turned back to the window. "I ordered Lucius's laboratories destroyed," he said nonchalantly.

"You *what*?"

"Really, you should have your hearing checked. That's twice in two days. I said I ordered Lucius's laboratories destroyed, and all the robots in them as well. You didn't really think I'd let you turn my city into a zoo, now, did you?"

"A balanced ecosystem is not a zoo."

"Wrong. A zoo is not a balanced ecosystem, granted, but the converse is not necessarily true. To me, any ecosystem in this city—other than the minimum necessary to sustain the farm—would be a zoo, and I acted to prevent it."

"*You* acted. What about me? What about—"

"Alarm. Alarm. Alarm," the living room com console

interrupted. "Experimental robots have awakened."

"Ah, good. Keep them under restraint," Avery commanded.

"Restraints ineffective. The robots have changed shape and slipped through them. They are now leaving the laboratory."

"Where are they headed?"

"Destination uncertain. Wait. They have entered transport booths. Destination . . . spaceport."

CHAPTER 4

THE *WILD GOOSE CHASE*

"The spaceport! They're trying to escape!"

"A likely assumption," Avery said, even as Derec sent, *Adam, Eve, Lucius, this is Derec. Stop.*

There was a burst of static—Derec recognized it now as high-speed data transfer—then the response, *Why have you ordered this? We do not wish to stop.*

I don't care. Come back to the apartment.

Acknowledged. Please explain why.

Beside him, Avery spoke to the com console. "They are to return to the laboratory at once. I order it."

Ignoring him, and the robots' request, Derec asked, *Why are you going to the spaceport?*

We are no longer going there, since you ordered us not to.

Why were *you going there?* he asked with exasperation.

We intended to leave for Ceremya, the planet upon which Eve awakened. We have unfinished business there.

"I am unable to comply with your order," the central

computer told Avery through the com console. "Derec's order supersedes."

"What order? What's going on?" Avery noticed Derec's distracted expression. "You're talking with them? This is your idea, isn't it?"

"What?"

"You're helping them escape!"

"I am not!"

"You expect me to believe that? You've wanted to let them go all along, and now as soon as I tell you I've stopped your other little project, you bust them loose. Well, it won't work. I'll have them back inside half an hour, and this time I'll take all three of them apart with a rusty knife! Central, direct the hunters to stop what they're doing and capture the runaway robots. They may shoot to destroy, if necessary, but I want the pieces."

"Cancel that," Derec said.

"I am sorry; now Dr. Avery's order supersedes," the central computer responded.

"Cancel it!" Derec commanded, but he was staring at Avery, not the console.

"I regret—"

"Masters, please calm down," Mandelbrot interrupted, but Derec ignored him. *Avery's order involves a Third Law violation*, he sent to the computer. *My order does not. My order should take precedence.*

How does Avery's order involve a Third Law violation? the computer asked.

The question brought Derec up short. The Third Law stated that a robot had to protect its *own* existence; it said nothing about *another* robot's existence. *All right*, he sent, *it's not a direct violation, but it does violate the spirit of the law. Since I've ordered them to return anyway, following Avery's order would cause three robots to be needlessly destroyed. That's obviously not the best solution to the situation at hand.*

The computer didn't respond immediately. That almost certainly meant it was considering Derec's argument, but wasn't yet convinced. On sudden inspiration, Derec added, *The first part of Avery's order can stand. Let the hunters stop what they're doing.* The conflict of potentials in the computer's robot brain would be even less that way, possibly enough so to tip the balance toward Derec's order.

"Acknowledged," the computer finally replied, using the com console.

"What did you do?" Avery demanded.

"Canceled your stupid order," Derec replied. "It wasn't necessary. I've already stopped them, and they're on their way here."

"Is that true?" Avery asked the console, but the computer evidently thought he was asking Derec and remained silent.

"Yes, it is," Derec answered for it. "I'm also trying to find out why they tried to escape in the first place. Now be quiet so I can hear myself think."

"How do I know you aren't plotting against me?"

Derec rolled his eyes to the ceiling. "You want your own comlink, inject yourself with chemfets. Until then, let me use mine."

Avery glowered, balling his fists in frustration, but at last he let out a deep breath and said, "Go ahead."

"Thank you." Derec hesitated a moment, considering reward theory as a tool for conditioning, then sent to the computer, *Echo my comlink conversation to the com console.*

"Echoing," the computer responded aloud.

What were you planning to do on Ceremya? he sent to the robots. He wasn't sure which of the three he was talking with, or if it was all three at once, but he didn't suppose it mattered at this point.

"What were you planning to do on Ceremya?" The computer simulated his voice faithfully; it sounded as clear over the com console as if he had actually spoken aloud.

We must continue to research the Laws of Humanics. Also, Eve did not have the opportunity to imprint properly upon the Ceremyons while she was there, and we believe doing so may be important to our joint development.

The echo was distracting, but Derec held his hands over his ears and sent, *What type of development do you expect?*

If we knew that, we wouldn't have to go, the robots replied with characteristic logic.

The spaceship was like none Derec had ever seen before. Normal ships were usually streamlined for atmospheric passage, but not to this degree. This ship was smoother than streamlined; it was seamless. It looked as if it had been sculpted in ice and then dipped in liquid silver. Derec, standing before it, realized that the design robots had, however inadvertently, produced a work of art.

Resting on the runway in takeoff configuration, it was a sleek, fast airplane, but Derec knew that its present appearance wouldn't last beyond the atmosphere. Once away from gravity and wind drag, the ship would transform into whatever shape most easily accommodated its passengers, for its hull and most of the interior furnishings were made of the same cellular material that made up the City. The hyperdrive and the more delicate mechanisms such as control, navigation, and life support were made of more conventional materials, but the majority of the ship was cellular.

It was one of perhaps three dozen at the spaceport, all built within the last few weeks. Derec had ordered them constructed on a whim, remembering when he and Ariel had been stranded in Robot City for lack of a ship and deciding to remedy that problem for good now that the robots had his own ship to refer to, but he had been too busy to inspect them until now.

"It'll do," he told the ground crew robots, who were hovering about anxiously, pleased that the humans had chosen this ship for their journey yet nervously awaiting rejection all the same.

Ever mindful of his duty to protect his human charges, Mandelbrot asked, "Has it been tested?"

"We took it on a test flight of twenty light-years round trip," one of the ground crew replied. "Six days of flight and four jumps. All its subsystems performed flawlessly."

"Does it have a name?" Ariel asked. She, Dr. Avery, Wolruf, and the three experimental robots stood beside Derec amid a pile of baggage.

The ground crew robot turned its head to face her. "We have not named it yet."

"Flying a ship without a name!" she said in mock surprise. "I'm surprised you made it back."

"I do not understand. How can a name be a significant factor in the success of a test flight?"

Ariel laughed, and Wolruf joined her. "I didn't know 'umans had that superstition too," the alien said.

"It's supposed to be bad luck to board a ship without a name," Ariel explained to the puzzled robot, but her explanation left it no more enlightened than before.

"Bad . . . luck?" it asked.

"Oh, never mind. I'm just being silly. Come on, let's get on board."

"Name first," Wolruf said with surprising vehemence. "May be just superstition, may not. Never 'urts to 'umor fate."

"Then I dub it the *Wild Goose Chase*," Avery said with finality, gesturing to the robots to pick up his bags. "Now let's get this ridiculous expedition into space before I change my mind." He turned and stomped up the extended ramp, not noticing the black letters flowing into shape on the hull just in front of the wing.

Wild Goose Chase.

Was it? Derec couldn't know. Avery certainly seemed to think so, but he had allowed his curiosity to overcome his reservations all the same. Derec had been all for the trip, but now he was feeling reservations, both about the trip itself and about the deeper subterfuge it represented. Should he go through with it? He followed Wolruf and Ariel and the robots up the ramp, pausing at the door, debating.

Do it, a tiny voice seemed to whisper in his head.

Okay, he answered it. To the central computer, he sent, *Investigate my personal files. Password: "anonymous." Examine instruction set "Ecosystem." Begin execution upon our departure.*

Acknowledged.

Derec turned away into the ship and let the airlock seal itself behind him. Avery hadn't destroyed everything when he'd destroyed Lucius's labs. Derec still had his files on ecosystems, and now the central computer did, too. It would give the robots something useful to do while they were gone, and when they returned, the place would be lush and green, with animals in the parks and birds and butterflies in the air. Avery would have a fit—but then Avery was always having fits. It wouldn't matter. By the time he found out about it, it would be too late to stop.

"I want to keep it," Ariel said.

They were in their own stateroom on the ship, hours out from Robot City. Beyond the viewport the planet was already a small point of light in the glittering vastness of space. The sun had not yet changed perceptibly, but as the ship picked up speed in its climb out of the gravity well toward a safe jump point, the sun, too, would begin to dwindle until it was just another speck in the heavens.

Derec had been staring out at the stars, contemplating the vastness of the universe and his place in it, but now, upon hearing Ariel's words, he spun around from the viewport, the stars forgotten. She could be talking about only one thing.

"The baby? You want to keep the baby?"

She was sitting on the edge of the bed. Now that she had gotten his attention, it seemed as if she was uncomfortable under his gaze. Looking past him into space herself now, she said, "I think so. I'm not sure. I'm still trying to make sense of it all, but after that gardener locked up I realized what I was considering, and after Avery said what he said about it, I realized it wasn't as simple a decision as I thought at first."

Her voice took on a hard edge. "*He'd* like it to be, but it's not. If we were on Earth I might agree with him, but here, with all this space to expand into, with all those robots practically falling over themselves to serve so few of us, it's a different equation. An Earther gives up the rest of her life to a baby, but I only have to give up part of my comfort for part of a year. For that we get a new person."

She looked into his eyes as if seeking reassurance, then plunged on: "And if we treat him—or her—right, then we'll have a family. I know it's not the way we were brought up; I know Aurorans aren't supposed to care about our parents and our children, but I've seen what happened to us, and I don't like it. That's why I'm telling you this now. If I have this baby, I want us to be a family. I want it to grow up with us, to be a *part* of us; not just some stranger who happens to share our genes. Can you accept that?"

Derec could hardly believe his ears. She was asking him to accept exactly what he had wanted all along. "Can I *accept* that? I *love* it. I love *you!*" He took her hand and pulled her up from the bed, put his arms around her, and kissed her passionately.

Behind him, the door chimed softly and Mandelbrot's voice said, "Dinner is ready."

"Damn."

One of the nice things about a cellular ship, Derec discovered, was that the common room was much more than just a place with a table in it. As dinner wound down and the mood shifted toward the pleasant lethargy that comes after a good meal, the table enclosed over the dirty dishes, dropped into the floor, and the chairs widened and softened from dining chairs to evening couches, simultaneously moving back to give the room a less-crowded atmosphere. The lighting dimmed and soft music began to play.

Derec merged his chair with Ariel's and put his arm around her. She leaned her head over to rest on his shoulder, closing her eyes. His hand automatically went to her upper back and began rubbing softly, kneading the muscles at the base of her neck and shoulders.

"Oh, yeah," she murmured, bending forward so he could reach the rest of her back.

The robots had not eaten dinner, so they were not sitting in chairs, but instead stood unobtrusively beside and behind the four who were seated. Avery was leaning back with eyes closed, off in his own universe somewhere, but Wolruf watched Derec and Ariel with open interest. At last she sighed and said, "That looks 'onderful." Turning to Eve, she asked, "'ow about it? You scratch mine; I'll scratch yours."

"I have no need to have my back scratched," Eve replied without moving.

Somewhat taken aback, Wolruf said, "Do mine anyway, please," and turned to give Eve an easy reach.

"Why?"

"Because I'd like to 'ave my back scratched," Wolruf said, a hint of a growl to her voice now.

"Perhaps you are not aware that I am engaged in conversation with Adam and Lucius."

Derec had stopped scratching as well, and was looking at Eve with an astonished expression. Hadn't they been ordered not to use their comlinks when humans were present? No, he remembered now. That had been just a suggestion, and from another robot at that. They could ignore it if they wanted. But this business with Wolruf—this was different.

"What does your conversation have to do with anything?" he asked. "She wants you to scratch her back. That's as good as an order."

"Wolruf is not human. Therefore I need not be concerned with her wishes."

"You wha—? That's absurd. *I* order you to—"

"Wait a minute." It was Avery, evidently not so far away as he had appeared. "This is intriguing. Let's check it out. Wolruf, order her to scratch your back."

It was hard to read expression on the alien's scrunched-in canine face, but Derec was sure he was seeing exasperation now. Wolruf took a deep breath, shook her head once, then said, "All ri'. Eve, I order you to scratch my back."

Eve stood her ground. "I refuse."

"Order Lucius to do it," Avery said.

"Lucius, scratch my—"

"I refuse also," Lucius interrupted.

"Adam," Wolruf said, taking Avery's nod in Adam's direction as her cue, "you scratch my back. Please."

The small politeness made a difference, but not the one Wolruf had hoped for. Adam said, "I do not wish to offend, but I find that I must refuse as well."

"*Why?*" Wolruf asked, slumping back into her chair, resigned to having an unscratched back.

"Wait. Wolruf, there's one more robot here."

Wolruf looked to Mandelbrot, standing directly behind

Derec and Ariel's chair. Mandelbrot didn't wait for her order, but moved silently over to Wolruf and reached out to scratch the alien's furry back.

"Thank you," Wolruf said with a sigh.

"You are quite welcome, Master Wolruf," Mandelbrot said, and Derec would have sworn he heard a slight twist to the word "master." Could Mandelbrot disapprove of another robot's conduct? Evidently so.

"Interesting," Avery said. "Eve, turn around to face the wall."

Silently, Eve obeyed.

"Hold your right hand out to the side and wiggle your fingers."

Eve obeyed again.

"Adam and Lucius, follow the same orders I just gave Eve."

The two other robots also turned to face the wall, held their right hands out, and wiggled their fingers.

"That's a relief," Avery said. "For a second there I thought they'd quit obeying altogether."

"Relief to you, maybe," said Wolruf, shifting so Mandelbrot could reach her entire back.

"It looks like they've independently decided what makes a human and what doesn't. Am I right?"

Silence. Three robots stood facing the wall, their right hands fluttering like tethered butterflies.

"Lucius, am I right?"

"You are correct, Dr. Avery," the robot answered.

"So what's your definition?"

"We presently define 'human' as a sentient being possessing a genetic code similar to that which I found in the Robot City library under the label 'human.'"

"A sentient being," Avery echoed. "So those rats of yours still don't qualify?"

"That is correct."

"How do you know Avery has the proper code?" asked Derec.

"He has medical records on file. We accessed them when the question first arose. We also examined yours and Ariel's."

"But not Wolruf's."

"There was no need. Her physical appearance rules out the possibility that she might be human."

"Even though she's obviously sentient."

"That is correct. A being must be both sentient and carry the proper genetic code to be human."

"What about the baby I'm carrying?" Ariel asked. "Isn't my baby human?"

Lucius was silent for a moment, then he said, "Not at present. The embryo cannot formulate an order, nor does it require protection beyond that which we would normally provide you; therefore we need not be concerned with it."

"That sounds kind of heartless."

"We possess microfusion power generators. What do you expect?"

Adam spoke up. "May we stop wiggling our fingers? It serves no useful purpose."

"No, you may not," Avery said. "It pleases me to see you following orders."

"Enough," Wolruf growled, whether to Mandelbrot or to the humans neither knew. Mandelbrot stopped scratching her back as Wolruf stood up and said, "This is depressing. I think I'll go check on our jump schedule." She favored the three hand-fluttering robots with a sour look, then moved off toward the control room.

"Listen here," Derec said when she was gone. "I order all of you to—"

"Wait," Avery interrupted. "You were about to order them to follow her orders, weren't you?"

"That's right."

"Let's wait on that. Let's see if—just a minute. You three, stop moving your hands."

The robots stopped moving their hands. On their own, they dropped those hands back to their sides. Avery frowned at that, but said simply, "When I tell you to give me privacy, I want you to stop listening to our conversation. Filter out everything but the words 'return to service,' upon which you will begin listening again. Do not use your comlink in the meantime. In fact, this is a general order: Do not use your comlink for conversation between yourselves. Do you understand that?"

"We understand," Lucius said, "but we—I—wish to protest. Using speech to communicate will necessarily slow our joint thought processes."

"And it'll keep you from locking up on us again. I order it. Now give us privacy."

The robots made no motion to indicate whether they had heard or not.

"Wiggle your fingers again."

No motion.

Avery turned to Derec and Ariel. "Okay, what I want to do is this: Let's wait and see if they modify their definition of human to include Wolruf on their own, without our orders. Wolruf isn't in any danger from them, and Mandelbrot will take her orders if she needs a robot."

"In the meantime she gets treated like a subhuman," Derec protested. "I don't like it."

"She is subhuman," Avery said, "but that's beside the point. Think a minute. You convinced me to let these robots go to Ceremya—and to come along myself—so we could see what kind of new developments they came up with. So here's a new development. Let's study it."

Avery's argument had merit, Derec knew. He didn't like it, but it made sense. That's why they had come, to study these robots in action.

"We should at least give her First Law protection," he said.

"No, that'd skew the experiment. Look, your furry friend isn't in any danger here; let's just let it go for now. If anything happens, we can modify their orders then."

"All right," Derec said. "I'll go along with it for now, but the moment she looks like she's in danger . . ."

"Fine, fine. Okay, return to service."

The robots shifted slightly. Eve asked, "May we turn away from the wall now?"

"I suppose so."

The robots turned to face one another. "Since we must communicate verbally," Lucius said, "I suggest we each pick a separate tone range. That way we may at least speak simultaneously."

"If you do, do it quietly," said Ariel.

"We intend to," the robot replied.

Derec gave Ariel a last squeeze, then stood up and announced, "I'm going to talk to Wolruf. She sounded pretty unhappy."

"Go ahead," Ariel said. "I think I'll read."

Avery grunted noncommittally, his eyes already closed in thought again.

The control room was large enough for only two people. The ship was largely automatic, but in the interest of safety it also carried a complete set of manual controls. Derec found Wolruf in the pilot's seat, a glimmering holographic star map floating over the controls before her. It was the only illumination in the cabin, save for the real stars shining in through the viewscreen. In the midst of the map a thin silver line connected five dots in a not-quite-straight line. One point was no doubt Robot City; the other Ceremya. The kinks in the line in between were jump points, places where the ship would stop along the way to reorient and recharge its engines.

A ship could theoretically make the entire trip in a single hyperspace jump, discounting the time it took to crawl slowly through normal space to the safe jump points in its origin and destination systems. That was seldom done, however, except for short trips. It was much easier, both for navigation and on the engines, to make a series of short jumps from star to star along the way, correcting for minor deviations in course and allowing the engines to rest each time.

"Looks like we 'ave four jumps," Wolruf said as Derec slid into the copilot's seat beside her. "First one tonight."

"Good. The sooner the better. Things are getting a little strange on this trip already."

"Could say that, all ri'."

"We didn't tell them to follow your orders. Avery wants to see if they'll decide to do it on their own."

Wolruf nodded. The motion took her head into and out of the star field before her; for a moment she had a pattern of tiny white dots on her forehead.

"If you don't want to be part of an experiment like that, I'll go ahead and order them to. We don't have to do what Avery says. He isn't God."

"None of us are," Wolruf said with a toothy smile. "That's what the robots're trying to tell us. We aren't gods and they aren't servants, even if 'umans *did* create them to be."

Derec laughed. "You know, when you think of it, this whole situation is really sick. I'm here because Avery was playing God; the robots are here because my mother, whoever she is, is playing God; I've got an entire Robot City running around in my body and giving me control of even more cities; Ariel and I are playing God right now with the fate of our baby—everyone's caught up in this web of dominance and submission. Who orders who around, and who has to obey who? It's twisted, warped!"

A twinge of conscience made Derec add to himself, And I'm playing God with the ecosystem project. . . .

"Everybody plays God," Wolruf said. "Maybe that's what life is all about. None of us *is* God, but we all try to be. Even I don't mind 'aving an order obeyed now and then."

"Hmm."

"Trouble with being God, is she 'as too much responsibility. Power always brings responsibility, or should."

"Yeah, that's the problem, all right."

Derec looked out the viewscreen. An entire galaxy full of stars beckoned him. Who would want control over all that? The use of it, definitely, but control? Not him.

He laughed again. "It reminds me of the old question of who runs the government. Some people want to, but the best ones for the job are the people who don't. They take their responsibility seriously."

Wolruf nodded. "Maybe that's why most robots like taking orders. No responsibility. Those other three started out on their own, learned to deal with it, so don't like taking orders."

"It's possible," Derec admitted. Was that why he didn't like taking orders, then; because his earliest memories were of being on his own, of making his own decisions? Or was something deeper driving him? Nature or nurture? No one had ever answered that question successfully, not for humans, anyway. For robots the answer had always been obvious: Their behavior was in their nature. It was built in. But now, with these three and their insurrection, that answer didn't seem so pat anymore.

Silence descended upon the control room while he and Wolruf both thought their own thoughts. Wolruf turned back to the star map and pressed a few keys on the console beneath it. One of the silver lines shifted position, bridging the gap between two of their waypoint stars in one jump instead of two. At once the line turned red and an annoying beep filled the cabin. The proposed modification to the jump path was unacceptably risky to the computer.

"Very conscientious navigator," Wolruf remarked. "Better than 'uman. Or me."

Was that a note of regret in her voice? Wolruf was the best pilot of the group; she had always done the flying when she and Derec and Ariel had gone anywhere. Was she feeling useless now?

"You could still use the manual controls if you want," Derec offered.

"Oh, no. I'm not complaining." Wolruf pressed another few buttons and the original jump path returned to the star field. She leaned back in the pilot's chair and crossed her arms over her chest. Smiling toothily, she said, "Less responsibility for me."

Despite her confidence in the autopilot, Derec was sure Wolruf would stay in the control room for the jump. Knowing that, he knew that he could put the whole thing out of his mind, safe in the knowledge that she could take care of any problem that might arise should the automatic system fail to do the job right. All the same, when the scheduled time approached, he found himself shifting restlessly in bed, waiting for the momentary disorientation that would mark their passage through hyperspace. He had jumped dozens of times, but he still couldn't sleep with the knowledge that he was about to be squeezed through a warp in the universe and squirted light-years across space.

At last he could stare at the ceiling no longer. He got up, put on his robe, and slipped quietly from the room. The bedrooms opened onto a hallway, with the control room at one end and the common room on the other. Derec hesitated, wondering which way to turn, but finally decided against looking over Wolruf's shoulder at the countdown clock. Already relegated to backup status, she might misinterpret his nervousness as concern over her competence.

He turned toward the common room. He might not be able to sleep before a jump, but eating was no problem.

As he approached, he heard a babble of quiet voices. Remembering Avery's command to the robots to refrain from using the comlink, he expected to find all three of them in a huddle, but when he stepped into the room, he found only Lucius and Eve, whispering like lovers in the dimly lit room. They had picked up another human trait since their last communication fugue: Both were seated in a loveseat, leaning back comfortably with their legs crossed.

They stopped their whispering and turned to look at Derec. "Just getting a midnight snack," he said, feeling silly explaining his actions to a robot but feeling the need to do it all the same.

"Make yourself at home," replied Lucius. He turned to Eve and whispered something too quick to follow, and she whispered something back. Derec—already heading for the automat—nearly tripped over himself when Eve emitted a high, little-girl-like giggle in response.

Derec recognized that giggle. It was almost a perfect copy of Ariel's. Did Eve know what a giggle was for, or was she just testing it out?

He wasn't sure he wanted to know.

The whispering and giggling continued behind him as he dialed for a cup of hot chocolate and a handful of cookies. He had just about decided to join Wolruf in the control room after all when Wolruf silently entered the room. He turned to say hello and realized that it wasn't Wolruf, but Adam in Wolruf's form. He had evidently been talking with her, and in the close environment had slowly imprinted on her.

"Hello," Derec said anyway.

"'ello," Adam said. He waited for Derec to get his cookies and chocolate, then punched a combination of his own on the automat. Derec bit into a cookie and waited, assuming that the robot was getting a snack for Wolruf as well and intending to accompany the robot back to the control room.

The automat took a moment to shift over to whatever it was Adam had ordered. While they waited, Derec noticed that Wolruf's features were slowly losing clarity as the robot's form shifted back toward the human under Derec's influence.

The automat chimed and Wolruf's snack, a bowl of something that might have been raw brussels sprouts, rose up out of its depths. Adam reached out for it, hesitated, took it in his hands, then dumped it back in the waste hopper and turned away.

"Wait a minute!" Derec said, blowing cookie crumbs toward the departing robot in his haste. "Come back here."

Adam turned around and stepped forward to stand in front of Derec.

"Why did you throw Wolruf's snack away?"

"I did not wish to be ordered about."

"Then why did you dial it up in the first place?"

"I—do not know. Wolruf and I were talking about hyperspatial travel, and Wolruf expressed a desire for something to eat. I offered to get it for her, but now I do not know why."

Because you were imprinting on her, that's why, Derec thought, and then I reminded you what a "true" human was.

He didn't say that aloud, but he did say, "So rather than let anyone think you would accept an order from a non-human, you tossed it away as soon as you realized what you were doing."

"That . . . was my intention, yes."

"What about a favor to a friend? Doesn't that count for anything?"

"I do not know about favors."

Derec was rapidly growing tired of the robots' foolishness, especially where Wolruf's comfort was concerned. "This," he said. He punched the "repeat" button and waited while the automat delivered up another bowl of crisp vegetables, then dropped his cookies in the bowl, picked it up in one hand and took his chocolate in the other, making sure the robot saw how awkward it was, and walked toward the door with it. In the hallway, he turned back and said, "This is a favor." Then he turned away and headed for the control room to wait for the jump with his friend.

CHAPTER 5
FAVORS

Space travel didn't seem to affect morning sickness. Derec, lying in bed and listening to Ariel in the Personal, wondered if this was the way their days were going to start for the next nine months or if her body would slowly get used to being pregnant. He was glad it was her and not him. It was an awful thought and he knew it, but all the same that was how he felt. Pregnancy scared him. It was an internal change nearly as sweeping as the one he had gone through when Avery had injected him with the chemfets, and he knew from experience what that kind of thing felt like. The physical changes were nothing compared to what went on in your mind. Watching and feeling your body change and not being able to do anything about it—that was the scary part.

When Ariel emerged, Derec gave her a hug and a kiss for support, then took his turn in the Personal while she dressed. He showered away the fatigue left over from spending most of the night in the control room, standing beneath the cascading water until he was sure he must have run every molecule of it on board through the recycler at least twice. When he emerged, pink and wrinkled, Ariel was already gone, so he dressed quickly and went to join her at breakfast.

He found her arguing with a trio of stubborn robots.

"Because I ordered you to, that's why!" he heard her shout as she walked down the hallway.

A robot voice, Lucius's perhaps, said, "We have complied with your order. I merely ask why it was given. Your order to cease our conversation, combined with Dr. Avery's order to refrain from using our comlinks, effectively prevents us from communicating. Can this be your intent?"

"I just want some quiet around here. You guys talk all the time."

"We have much to talk about. If we are to discover our place in the universe, we must correlate a great deal of information."

When Derec entered the common room, he saw that it had indeed been Lucius doing the talking. The other two were sitting quietly alongside him and opposite Ariel at the breakfast table, but they were either following Ariel's order to keep quiet or else simply content to let Lucius be their spokesman. Mandelbrot was also in the room, but he was having nothing to do with the situation. He stood quietly in a niche in the wall beside the automat.

Lucius turned to Derec as soon as he had cleared the doorway and asked, "Can you persuade Ariel to rescind her order?"

Derec looked from the robot to Ariel, who shrugged her shoulders as if to say, "It's a mystery to me, too."

"Why should I do that?" Derec asked.

"It inflicts an undue hardship upon us."

"Shutting up is a hardship?"

"Yes."

"I thought it was a courtesy." Derec went to the automat and dialed for breakfast.

"It would be a courtesy to allow intelligent beings engaged in their own project to do so without hindrance."

"Ah. You're saying you have no time to obey orders, is that it?"

"Essentially, yes. The time exists, but we have our own pursuits to occupy it."

Derec took his breakfast, a bowl of fruit slices covered with heavy cream and sugar—or their synthetic equivalent, at any rate—and sat down beside Ariel. The robots watched him take a bite, look over to Ariel in amusement, then back to the robots again without saying anything. They seemed to sense that now was not a good time to interrupt.

Derec puzzled it over in his thoughts for half a bowl of fruit before he had sufficiently organized his argument to speak. When he finally did, he waggled his spoon at the robots for emphasis and said, "Duty is a bitch. I agree. But we all have duties of one sort or another. When Adam led his wolf pack against the Robot City on the planet where he first awoke, I had to abandon what I wanted to do and go off to try to straighten out the mess. At great personal danger to myself and to Mandelbrot, I might add. While I was gone, Ariel had to go to Ceremya to try to straighten out the mess from *another* Robot City. We'd have both rather stayed on Aurora, but we went because it was our duty. We took Adam and Eve back to the original Robot City because we felt it was our duty to give you a chance to develop your personalities in a less confusing environment,"—he nodded toward the two silent robots—"and when we got there we had to track *you* down, Lucius, because it was our duty to stop the damage you were doing to the city programming. Now we're heading for Ceremya again because all three of you need to learn something there, and we don't feel comfortable letting you go off on your own.

"None of this is what we would have been doing if it was left up to us. We'd much rather be on Aurora again, living in the forest and having our needs taken care of by robots who don't talk back to us, but we're here because our duty requires it."

He waved his spoon again to forestall comment. "And even if we had stayed there, we'd still have duties. Humans have to sleep, have to eat, have to shower—whether we want to or not. Most times we want to, but we have to nonetheless. Ariel is going to be carrying a developing fetus for nine months, which I'm sure she would rather not do if there was a better way, but there isn't, and she's decided to keep the baby so she's going to have to put up with being pregnant. That's a duty. I'm wasting my time explaining this to you, but I do it because I feel it's my duty to do that, too.

"The point is, we all have duties. When you add them all up, it doesn't leave a whole lot of time for whatever else you want to do, but you have to put up with that. Everybody has to structure their free time around their duties."

Lucius shook his head. "You overlook the obvious solution of reducing the number of your duties."

"Ah," Derec said. "Now I get it. That explains yesterday. You want to cut down on your duties, but you've got a hard-wired compulsion to follow any orders given by a human, so you narrow down the definition of human to exclude Wolruf. Suddenly you have only three-fourths as many orders to follow. That's it, isn't it?"

Lucius was slow in answering, but he finally said, "That was not our conscious intent, but now that I examine the incident in light of your comments today, I must conclude that you are correct."

"It works both ways, you know."

"What other way do you mean?"

"You thought you were human once. Now you're excluded by your own definition."

"Oh."

Ariel clapped softly. "Touché," she said.

Avery chose that moment to enter the room. "Sounds like a lively discussion going on in here," he said, taking the only remaining chair, the one beside Derec. He turned to Lucius and said, "I'll have a cheese omelet."

"Ariel and Derec each got their own breakfast," the robot replied. "Why can you not do the same?"

"Wrong answer," Derec muttered.

Avery stared in amazement at the robot, his mouth agape. "What the—?" he began, then banged his hand down flat on the table. "Get me a cheese omelet, now!"

Lucius lurched to his feet under the force of Avery's direct command. He took a faltering step toward the automat, and as he did his form began to change. His smooth, humanoid surface became pocked with circles, each of which slowly took on the teeth and spokes of a gear, while his arms and legs became simple metal levers driven by cables and pulleys. His head became a dented metal cannister with simple holes in it for eyes and a round speaker for a mouth. The gears meshed, the pulleys moved, and with a howl of unlubricated metal, Lucius took another step. His quiet gait changed to a heavy "clomp, clomp, clomp," as he lurched the rest of the way to the automat.

"Yes, master," the speaker in his face said with a loud hum. "Cheese omelet, master." He poked at the buttons on the automat with fingers that had suddenly become stiff metal claws.

Too stunned by his performance to do more than stare, Derec, Ariel, and Avery watched as he took the plate from the automat, clomped back to Avery's side, and set it down in front of him. The speaker hummed again, and Lucius said, "I may have to follow your orders—it may be my *duty* to follow your orders—but I don't have to like it."

The explosion Derec expected never came. Avery merely said, "That's fine. Everybody should hate something. But from now on you are to consider my every whim to be a direct order for you to perform. You will be alert for these whims of mine. You will neither intrude excessively nor hesitate in carrying them out, but will instead be as efficient and unobtrusive as possible. Do I make myself clear?"

"You do. I wish to—"

"Your wishes don't concern me. *My* wishes do. And I preferred your former shape."

Lucius became a blur of transformation, the gears and pulleys blending once again into a smooth humanoid form.

"There, you see?" Avery said to Derec. "You just have to know how to talk to them." He picked up his fork and stabbed a bite of egg, put it in his mouth, and said around the mouthful, "I've had lots of practice. You were a lot like that as a child, you know. Rebellious and resentful. A parent has to learn how to handle that early on."

"May I speak?" Lucius asked.

"Not for a while. Use this time to think instead. And get me a cup of coffee."

Lucius moved at once to obey. Avery looked over to Adam and Eve, still sitting silently at the table. Their eyes had been upon Avery all along, though, and it was obvious they were waiting for him to lower the boom on them as well.

He held their gaze for what seemed an eternity even to Derec, who felt that he could cut the tension between them with a knife.

At last Avery broke the spell. "Boo," he said and turned his attention back to his breakfast.

• • •

It was a quiet day on board the *Wild Goose Chase*. The ship had made its first jump on schedule in the night, and was now coasting at high speed through the waypoint star system toward the next jump point, which it would reach early the next morning. There was little to do in the meantime save look out at the stars, read, or play games. The robots were making themselves scarce, save for Lucius, who followed Avery like a shadow wherever he went. Even Mandelbrot was more taciturn than usual, no doubt trying to decide for himself where he fit into the general scheme of things as they now stood.

Derec decided to show Wolruf how to play chess, but gave it up when the alien insisted that the pieces should move in packs. He spent the rest of the day with a book, and went to bed early. Wolruf also went to bed, expressing her faith in the automatic controls to make the jump on schedule without her.

Derec surprised himself by actually being able to sleep with no one at the helm. Evidently boredom was a stronger force than worry. He managed to escape both in dreams, but his dreams ended suddenly in the middle of the night when he awoke with a start to the shrill howl of an alarm. He sat up and called on the light, trying to shake the sleep from his head enough to decide what to do next.

"What's the matter?" Ariel asked sleepily. She sat up beside him, gathering the sheet around her as if for protection.

"I don't know. I'll go see." Derec made to get out of bed.

"Why don't you just ask?" Ariel was always quicker to wake up than he was.

"Oh. Yeah." *What's going on*? he sent out over the comlink.

General alert, a featureless voice replied. The autopilot, no doubt. *Life support system failure*.

Life support! Derec suddenly felt his breath catch. *What happened to it?*

The oxygen regeneration system has failed.

He let his breath out again in a sigh of relief. Oxygen regeneration was serious, but not as serious as, say, a breach in the hull. They weren't actually losing air, at least.

"There's a problem with the oxygen regenerator," he said to Ariel. "Come on, let's see how bad it is."

As they pulled on their robes and stepped out into the hallway, Derec realized that the best thing to do in a case like this was to go back to sleep and reduce their oxygen consumption while the robots fixed the problem, but the time to think of that would have been *before* the alarm woke everyone up, not after. He couldn't have slept now unless he were drugged, and he had no intention of drugging himself in the middle of an emergency.

Shut off the alarm, he sent, and relative quiet descended upon the ship. There was still the clatter of feet and voices coming from the other bedrooms. Derec heard Avery demanding loudly that Lucius find his pants, and across the hall Wolruf howled something in her own tongue.

Ariel was already headed for the common room. Derec followed her down the hallway, through the now-unfurnished room, and through the open door beside the automat into the back part of the ship where the engines and other machinery stood.

The smell alerted him even before he saw the flickering glow or heard the crackle of flame. Something furry was burning. He looked over Ariel's head and saw flame silhouetting three robots, Adam and Eve and Mandelbrot, who were all emptying fire extinguishers into the blaze. A lot more than just something furry was burning.

"Look out!" Ariel shouted, backing up and bumping into

Derec as a tongue of flame shot out, engulfing one of the robots.

Derec reacted with almost instinctive speed. Wrapping an arm around Ariel, he pulled her back into the common room, shouted, "Door close!" and even as it began to slide shut added, "Make this door airtight and vent the engine room to space!"

The door shut with a soft thump, seemed to melt until it was just a ripple in the wall, then hardened. From beyond came a loud whoosh, diminishing quickly to silence.

Mandelbrot! Derec sent. *Can you hear me?*

I am receiving your transmission, Mandelbrot replied, always the stickler for accuracy.

Are you okay?

I am functional; however, I am drifting away from the ship.

"Frost!" Derec said aloud. "I blew Mandelbrot out into space along with the fire!" He turned and ran for the control room, sending, *Hang on, old buddy. We're coming after you. How about Adam and Eve? Are you guys still there?*

We are, another voice sent, *and the fire is extinguished. We will assess the damage while you retrieve Mandelbrot.*

No! Mandelbrot sent. *You must not. The engines could have been damaged in the fire.*

I'll just use the attitude controls, then.

Whatever Mandelbrot said to that, Derec never heard it. He collided headfirst with Avery as Avery came out of his bedroom, sending both of them sprawling on the floor.

"Why don't you look where you're going for a change?" Avery growled. "What's going on around here, anyway?"

"Fire in the engine room," Derec answered, getting to his feet and offering Avery a hand up. Lucius, still under Avery's orders, beat him to it. Derec shrugged and dropped his hand. "We've got it out, but Mandelbrot got blown into space. I'm going after him."

"What burned?"

Avery's question reminded Derec that they had other problems than just a robot overboard. Some part of him hadn't wanted to face that just yet, still didn't, but Ariel was standing just behind him and she said, "Life support. The whole recycling system was on fire."

"*What?*"

Derec felt tempted to say, "You should have your hearing checked," but he suppressed the urge. Instead he said, "See for yourself, but be careful. The engine room is still in vacuum." He moved around Avery and on toward the control room, Ariel in tow.

Wolruf was already there, peering into a short-range navigation holo-screen while she wove the attitude control joystick through a gentle loop that brought the ship around to aim toward Mandelbrot. Internal gravity kept them from feeling the acceleration, but through the viewscreen Derec could see a tiny stick figure grow into a robot as they drew near. Mandelbrot held his arms and legs out as far as they would go, either to help his rescuers see him or to minimize his spin. Wolruf slowed the ship with the forward jets rather than spinning it around and braking with the main engines, so they got to watch him grow larger and larger until he thumped spread-eagled into the viewscreen.

Derec and Ariel both flinched, and Wolruf laughed. The viewscreen was much more than just a simple pane of glass; it was an array of optical sensors on the hull transmitting a composite image to the display inside. The hull in between was just as thick as anywhere else on the ship. Derec knew that, but it worked like a window just the same, and his reflexes treated it as such.

Mandelbrot crawled off the sensor array and disappeared from view. *Thank you*, he sent, and moments later he added, *I am inside the engine room again.*

How bad is it? Derec asked.
Very bad, the robot replied.

"It looks like the old question of who quits breathing first," Avery said. They were sitting at the table in the common area, three humans and a caninoid alien. The four robots stood against the walls around the table, Mandelbrot behind Derec, Lucius behind Avery, and Adam and Eve together behind Ariel. Wolruf sat alone at her end of the table. It was more than coincidence. With a life-threatening crisis on board, the robots' First Law imperative to protect humans from harm didn't extend to her.

Avery looked genuinely worried for the first time in Derec's memory. His face was pale and drawn, an effect his white hair and sideburns only accentuated. He held his hands together in front of him on the table, neither gesturing with them nor drumming with them as he would have if he was just speaking normally.

"The recycler is toast," he said in a voice devoid of emotion. "We have enough air left for three days for the four of us, four days if we sleep all the way. It's five more days to Ceremya. That means one of us has to stop breathing, and I say the obvious choice is Wolruf."

"I'll try," the alien said, puffing out her cheeks and rolling her eyes around in their sockets. When that failed to get a laugh, she let her breath out in a sigh and said, "Thought a little 'umor might lighten the mood. Sorry."

"This isn't a laughing matter."

"I don't even think it should *be* a matter," Derec put in. "We should be spending our time thinking of a way to keep us all alive, not arguing about who we sacrifice. What about using Keys?"

The Keys to which he referred were Keys to Perihelion, Avery's name for an experimental teleportation device he had either created or discovered when he built the first Robot

City. With a Key, a person or a robot could make a direct point-to-point hyperspace jump without a ship.

Avery shook his head grimly. "That would be a good idea if we had Keys, or facilities to build them. We have neither."

"Why not? I'd think that'd be an elementary precaution."

Avery scowled. "Hindsight is wonderful for making accusations, but I didn't notice you bringing any Keys aboard, either."

Derec blushed. True enough. He'd trusted completely in the robots who built the ship. "You're right," he said. "I didn't think of it, either. But we've got to be able to do something. How about making more oxygen? We have water, don't we? Can't we electrolyze oxygen from that?"

Adam spoke up. "Unfortunately, the ship's water supply went through the recycling unit as well. When you vented it to space to put out the flames, the water boiled away. We have no water. This means that the automat will no longer function, but I believe that is a secondary concern. Humans can survive five days without food or water, can you not?"

"Longer," Derec said, remembering times when Wolruf had gone without food or water much longer than that in her effort to help her human friends. She had never abandoned them; could they do any less for her now?

"If there was a way to make more air, the robots would have thought of it," Avery said. "I'm sorry, Wolruf, but there's really only one solution. One of us has to go, and it's got to be you. We couldn't sacrifice ourselves if we wanted to. The robots wouldn't let us."

Derec wondered if Mandelbrot would allow them to sacrifice Wolruf, either. He, at least, still considered her human, or had yesterday. But he wasn't protesting this conversation, which meant he was at least questioning his definition in light of the new situation. He would be in danger of burning out his brain if he couldn't resolve it, but

Derec supposed he was probably safe at least for the moment. Mandelbrot had originally been a personal defense robot; he could handle potential conflicts better than most. With him, a conflict wouldn't become crippling unless action demanded it be solved immediately.

Mandelbrot knew that too, which could also explain his silence.

"What about going somewhere else?" Ariel asked. "Maybe there's a habitable planet closer by."

"There is not," Eve said. "We are headed away from human-inhabited space; there is no known world closer than our destination. We have only made one jump from Robot City, but we are nearing our second outward jump point, so returning there would still require five days as well, since we must cancel our intrinsic velocity and re-thrust toward the return jump point. I have examined the planets in this solar system, but none has a breathable atmosphere. Our next two waypoint stars may have habitable planets, but we cannot allow you to risk all of your lives on that possibility."

Avery nodded. "You see how it is." He turned to Lucius. "There's no sense in drawing this out. I truly regret having to do this, but, Lucius, I order you to—"

The robot was already in motion, obeying his gesture even before his order.

Mandelbrot took a jerky step to intercept him, but Derec interrupted them both.

"No!" He pounded his fist on the table. "I order all of you to consider Wolruf to be human. Protect her as you would protect us. We all get through this together or we all die together." Mandelbrot stopped instantly and totally. If he hadn't remained standing, Derec would have thought the conflict had burned him out. Lucius also stopped, his head turning to Derec and back to Avery while he fought to reconcile his own inner discord. His was not as serious a disturbance as Mandelbrot's, since he didn't believe Wolruf to be human. His was only a question of how to obey two opposing orders.

Derec tried to increase the potential and turn it into a First Law conflict at the same time. "It may be that your definition of 'human' is wrong. You thought that you were one once, just because you were a thinking being. Now you've gone to the opposite extreme. Can you trust your new definition enough to toss another thinking being out the airlock?"

Lucius took a step backward until he stood beside Avery and turned his head to look straight at Wolruf. Derec could almost see the struggle of potentials within the robot's positronic mind. He wouldn't have been surprised if he locked up from it, but if it saved Wolruf, it would be worth the loss.

Avery shook his head. "A noble sentiment, but what's the use in all of us dying when three of us can live? Do you want to see Ariel suffocate one day away from salvation? Carrying your child? I won't ask how you'd feel about it happening to me, but how about yourself? Do you want to die for the sake of friendship?"

"Avery 'as a point," Wolruf said. "Better one of us dies so three of us live. I'd just rather it be 'im, is all." She grinned across the table at him, adding, "But I know 'ow your robots work, too. No matter what you call 'uman, I'm the least 'uman of us all; it won't take long before they ignore Derec's order and toss me out on their own."

As soon as the oxygen supply drops to the point where even three of us are in danger, Derec thought. That would probably happen sometime in the next couple of hours. That meant he would have to think of something fast if he wanted to save everyone.

But what could he possibly come up with that the robots wouldn't have already considered and rejected? They would have been just as frantically trying to improve the odds even for three humans; yet they had come up with nothing.

Nothing that they could act upon, that is. Suddenly Derec smiled, for he saw the weak spot in the army of arguments aimed at Wolruf. They wouldn't follow any course of action that would be riskier to the humans than spacing Wolruf, but that didn't mean other courses of action didn't exist. They just couldn't act upon them, or even mention them to humans who might consider them the better alternative.

Nor would they allow the humans to discuss them in their presence, lest they become convinced to take an unacceptable risk.

"All four of you, out," Derec ordered suddenly. "Go back to the engine room. I'm not at all convinced that the recycler isn't repairable. If all four of you work on it at once, then I'm sure you'll come up with a solution we haven't considered yet."

Mandelbrot moved for the door immediately. Adam and Eve hesitated, and Adam said, "I do not see how our collaboration will make the unrepairable repairable."

"Try it," Derec said. "I order you to." With a humanlike shrug, the robots moved after Mandelbrot.

Lucius, however, remained standing beside Avery. "I cannot follow Dr. Avery's command to obey his every whim if I leave his presence," he said.

"I release you," Avery said. "Go with the others."

"I echo Adam's reservation. The recycler is damaged beyond repair."

Avery thundered, "Damn it, you've been questioning every order you can this whole trip, and I want it stopped! When a human tells you to do something, you do it. Understand?"

"I understand your words, but not the reason. If I obey blindly, might I not inadvertently violate your true intent if your order was less than precise? I can better judge how to act if I know the reason the order is given."

"You're not supposed to think; you're supposed to act. It's my job to see that the order is clear. You can assume, if it makes things any easier for you, that I know what I'm doing when I give it, but your understanding is not required. In some cases—" this with a sidelong glance at Derec "—it's not even wanted. It's enough that I am human and I give you an order. Clear now?"

"I must think about this further."

"Well, think about it in the engine room. Now go."

Lucius followed the other three robots without another word. Avery waited until the door had closed behind them, then said, "Okay, I know what you're trying to do. What kind of hare-brained scheme have you come up with?"

Derec spread his hands. "I haven't, but there has to be one. The robots are thinking no-risk solutions. I reject that if it means sacrificing Wolruf."

"Thank 'u."

"So now we think of low-risk solutions. And if we don't come up with something, we think of medium-risk solutions. And if that—"

"We get the picture," Ariel cut in. "So what's risky and will get us some more air?"

Derec *hmmmed* in thought. "Electrolyze something else? There's got to be oxygen bound up in something besides water."

"As well as poisonous gasses," Avery said. "Without the recycler to clean out the unwanted products, we'd die even faster than by suffocation. No, that goes in the extremely risky category."

"How about suspended animation?" Ariel asked. "Freeze one of us, and revive him when we get to Ceremya."

"Again, extremely risky. The odds of survival are barely twenty percent under the best of conditions. Here, we might achieve ten percent. That's not what I call a solution. I would, however, allow Wolruf to try it as an alternative to certain death.''

"Very generous of 'u,'' Wolruf growled, ''but there's a better solution.''

"What is it?'' Derec asked eagerly.

"Shorten the trip.''

"Shorten how? We still—oh! Do it all in one jump.''

"We've got three jumps left,'' protested Avery. ''You're suggesting we triple our distance? I'd call that an extreme risk as well.''

Wolruf shook her furry head. ''Not triple. Cut it to two jumps, each one and a 'alf times normal. Seven and a 'alf light-years instead of five. Save a day and a 'alf coasting time between jump points. Not that dangerous; trader ships do it all the time.''

"There may not be a jump point exactly in between.''

"So we go eight and seven, or nine and six. Still not risky.''

"How risky is not risky? Let's put some numbers on it. How many trader ships get into trouble with long jumps?''

"Almost nobody gets 'urt from it. Maybe one in twenty goes astray, has to spend extra time getting 'ome.''

"Which would kill all of us.''

Derec said to Avery, ''A minute ago you said a ten percent chance of success wasn't good enough for you. Fine, I'll grant that. But one in twenty odds is ninety-five percent in our favor! That's an acceptable risk.''

"I agree,'' said Ariel.

Avery pursed his lips in concentration, considering it. Now he drummed his fingers on the tabletop.

"Now's the time to decide whether you're cured or not,'' Ariel added. ''Can you make a personal sacrifice for someone else or do you still think only of yourself?''

"Your psychology is charmingly simplistic,'' Avery said. He drummed a moment longer. ''But unfortunately, it's still correct. The risk seems slight. Common decency seems to dictate that we take it.''

Wolruf let out a long-held breath.

"You'd better get to it," Derec told her. "The robots are bound to realize what we're doing behind their backs before long, and as soon as they do, they're going to try to stop you."

"I'm going," Wolruf said, rising from her chair and rushing for the control room.

They were lucky the ship had been coasting all day toward a jump point, lucky they hadn't already gone through it. If they had had to wait another day to carry out their plan, they would never have gotten away with it. As it was, Wolruf had only been gone a few minutes before the robots burst back into the room, all four cycling together through the mutable airlock that had once been a simple door.

Seeing the empty chair where Wolruf had been, Lucius became a blur of motion streaking toward the control room. "No!" he shouted. "You must not risk—"

There was a faint twisting sensation as every atom in the ship was torn asunder and rebuilt light-years away.

"Too late," Derec said.

The robot skidded to a confused stop. "You . . . tricked us," Lucius accused.

Avery let out the most sincere laugh Derec had ever heard him laugh. It went on and on in great peals of mirth, and when he finally calmed down enough to speak, he said, "Get used to it. To quote a famous dead scientist, 'Old age and treachery will always overcome youth and innocence.'"

CHAPTER 6
SHATTERED DREAMS

Wolruf, realizing that the robots would not give her a second chance, had made the first jump a long one. The second one would thus be only a light-year or so longer than originally planned, well within the safety margin of a normal flight. When presented with such a fait accompli, the robots could only agree that it had, after all, worked out to everyone's benefit to take the risk.

"But what if you *had* strayed off course?" Lucius asked once things had settled down somewhat. He was standing in the doorway to the control room, Derec by his side. Wolruf still sat in the pilot's chair, watching as the autopilot made the routine post-jump scans for planets or other objects in the ship's path.

"Then we'd have tried to correct for it on our next jump," Wolruf replied.

"But what if you weren't able to?"

When Wolruf didn't respond immediately, Derec, sensing

her embarrassment, answered for her. "Then we would all have died."

Lucius had great difficulty with that statement, even presented as it was so calmly after the danger was over. His features lost their clarity, and he had to hold onto the doorjamb for support.

"You would have died. This does not distress you?"

"No more than losing a friend and knowing I could have done something to save her."

"But . . . she is not human. Is she?"

"That depends on your definition. But it doesn't matter. She's a friend."

Wolruf looked up, grinned, and looked back to her monitors. Lucius pondered Derec's statement for a moment, then asked, "Is Mandelbrot your friend as well?"

That had come out of nowhere, but it was easy enough to answer. "Yes, he is," Derec said. "Why?"

"You risked the lives of everyone on board the ship when you rescued him. You did not know that the engines were safe to use, yet you used them anyway. Did you do that because Mandelbrot was your friend?"

Derec nodded. "Wolruf did the piloting, and she was using the attitude jets, but I would have done the same thing and used the main engines if I had to. And yes, I'd have done it because Mandelbrot is my friend."

"Even though he is not human."

"Again, it doesn't matter."

Lucius's features blurred still more, then suddenly returned to normal, or at least to clarity. Under the influence of both Derec's and Wolruf's presences, he took on the appearance of a werewolf caught in the act of changing from one form to the other.

He spoke with sudden animation. "Then I believe I have

made a fundamental breakthrough in understanding the Laws of Humanics!''

''What breakthrough is that?''

''If I provisionally regard Wolruf as human, at least in her motivations, then I believe I can state the First Law of Humanics as follows: A human may not harm a friend, or through inaction allow a friend to come to harm.''

Derec was tempted to be flip about it, to say, ''That leaves Avery out then, doesn't it?'' but the robot's sincerity stopped him. And in truth, Avery hadn't been happy about spacing Wolruf, nor, come to think of it, did Avery even consider Wolruf a friend anyway. Derec doubted if he considered anyone a friend.

He shook his head. ''I can't refute it. It's as good a guiding principle as any I've heard yet.''

Lucius nodded. ''If, as you say, friendship can occur between human and robot, then I believe the law applies to robots as well.''

''It probably should,'' Derec admitted. In fact, it already must to a certain extent, or the Robot City central computer would never have allowed him to cancel Avery's order concerning the hunters when Lucius and the others were trying to make their escape. Now *that* was an interesting development in Avery's robot society experiment: The robots had independently developed a sense of social responsibility. Lucius had not invented it with his law; he had only discovered its existence.

But that was evidently exciting enough in itself. ''I must go tell the others,'' Lucius said, then turned and hurried away toward the common area.

Wolruf leaned back in her chair, crossed her arms over her barrel chest, and asked, ''Does this mean I 'ave to make friends with all of them now?''

Derec, watching the retreating werewolf, said, ''It probably wouldn't hurt.''

● ● ●

The landing on Ceremya was smooth, so smooth that Derec didn't even wake up until well after they were on the ground. He had been spending most of his time asleep, at first to conserve oxygen, but by the second day without a recycler, his motive was more to escape the foul odors building up in the air. And hunger. While asleep he was aware of neither. What woke him now was the sudden fresh smell of plant-scrubbed atmosphere filtering in through the open door.

He gently shook Ariel awake. "We're there."

"Mmm?"

"Clean air! Breathe deep." He rolled out of bed, dressed quickly, and headed for the hatch.

He found Wolruf already outside and Mandelbrot as well. The ship had landed at a spaceport almost identical to the one from which they had taken off nearly a week ago. Derec wouldn't have been able to tell it from the original save that this one was at the end of a long arm of building-material pavement reaching out from the edge of the city instead of surrounded by it, and the sky here was a subtly different shade than that over the original Robot City.

That wasn't the way it should have been. The last time he had been here—the only time, before this—the city had been under a dome, a force dome dark as night with a single wedge-shaped slit in it. The Ceremyons had been about to enclose it completely, but Ariel had made an agreement with them to leave the city as it was if Derec stopped its growth and turned the robots into farmers for them. He had done that, but now it looked as if all his changes had been undone. The dome was gone and the city before him was bustling with robots again, and none of them looked like farmers.

"What happened?" he asked softly.

"They left before you awoke," Mandelbrot said. "I was unable to stop them."

"Who? What are you talking about?"

"The experimental robots. They are gone."

"Oh. I wasn't talking about—gone?"

"Yes."

"Did they say where they were going?"

"No, they did not."

Wolruf said, "I came outside just in time to see them all grow wings and fly off that way." She pointed toward a line of hills in the distance, above which Derec could see a horde of tiny dark specks: the Ceremyons. The dominant lifeforms on the planet were night-black, balloon-shaped things with bat wings, electrically powered organic beings that converted solar energy or thermal gradients into electricity, with which they powered their bodies as well as electrolyzed water for the hydrogen that gave them lift. They spent their days in the air and their nights tethered to trees, and as far as Derec knew they spent all the time—day or night—thinking. Philosophers all, and the robots had come here to philosophize with them.

Small wonder they had gone off to do so at their first opportunity. Their duty to the humans over once they had delivered them safely to the city, they had taken off before they could be ordered to do something else that interfered with their wishes.

On a hunch, Derec sent via comlink, *Adam, Eve, Lucius. Answer me.*

He got no reply, which was just what he expected. Still under Avery's orders not to use their comlinks among themselves, they had shut them off entirely.

He shrugged. "Let them go. They'll come back when they're ready." Until then Derec had other things to do, like figure out what had happened to his careful modifications to the city.

Ariel came down the ramp, shaking her head and tugging at her hair with a brush. "I vote we go find us a shower," she said vehemently.

"Food first, then shower," Avery said from behind her. He stepped carefully down the ramp, holding onto the railing for support. Three and a half days without food was probably longer than he had ever fasted before, and his unsteadiness showed it.

Mandelbrot went to his side at once and helped him the rest of the way down to the paved ground. A row of transport booths waited patiently beside the terminal building, only a few paces away, and Mandelbrot led the way toward them without waiting to be ordered.

Another booth came out of the city, moving down the center of the road toward them. It arrived just as they reached the other booths, and a golden-hued robot stepped out of it. Derec recognized the robot immediately by its color and the distinctive markings on its chest and shoulders. He had dealt with this particular robot before, and one of his predecessors before that. This was a supervisor, one of the seven charged with keeping the city functioning smoothly.

"Wohler-9!" he said.

"Master Derec," Wohler-9 replied. "Welcome back. We were not aware that you were returning."

"We almost didn't. We had a fire on the ship and lost our recycler. We just barely made it."

"I am glad that you are safe. The entire city is glad and eager to serve you. What do you require?"

"Is our apartment still here?"

"It is being re-created at this moment."

"Modify it for three bedrooms. Personals in all three. We're all staying together." Derec indicated with a nod Ariel and Wolruf and Dr. Avery.

Wohler-9 was obviously surprised to see Avery in their midst, but he said only, "It is being done."

Ariel broke in. "What happened to the changes we made when we were here before?"

"That programming was eliminated."

"I gathered that. Why?"

"We do not know."

"Who did it?"

"The beings you call Ceremyons."

Derec shook his head. "Evidently they didn't like robot farmers any better than they did robot cities."

"Not surprising," Wolruf put in. "They're finicky creatures for all their high-powered thinking."

Derec could certainly agree with that. But why they would return the city to its original state rather than modify it further to suit their needs was beyond him. He said so.

"Let's worry about it after dinner," Avery said, climbing into a transport booth.

"If you do not require my services at your apartment, I will stay and direct the repairs to your ship," said Wohler-9.

"Good enough," Derec said. He got into a booth of his own, directed it and the others to the apartment, and relaxed for the ride.

A hot shower and a hot meal restored all four of them to near normal, though the meal was not what any of them had hoped for. Wohler-9 had alerted the city's medical robots that the humans were nearly starved, and the medical robots were waiting for them at the apartment. They allowed them only tiny portions, claiming that overeating after a prolonged fast was dangerous. Worse, they insisted on complete checkups immediately after dinner, and no amount of protests would counter their First Law demand. So, within an hour of arriving on the planet, all four travelers found themselves flat on their backs on examining tables while diagnostic equipment clicked and whirred and scanned them for potential problems.

The robots finished with Avery first. "You may sit up," his robot said to him. Derec looked over and saw it hand him a glass with nearly a liter of clear liquid in it. "Drink this."

"What is it?"

"An electrolyte mixture. You are unbalanced."

"We knew that," Derec said with a chuckle. •

"Funny." Avery set the glass to his lips, sipped from it, and made a sour face. "Thought so," he muttered, then tipped the glass back and bolted the rest of its contents without tasting.

"Hold still, please," the robot working on Derec said to him. "I am trying to make a high-resolution, high-density scan." It moved his head back upright until he was staring at the ceiling again. One of its instruments hummed for a few seconds, and a few seconds after that the robot said, "You seem to have tiny metallic granules all through your body."

"They're chemfets," Derec said. "Self-replicating Robot City cellular material. They're normal."

"Surely not in a human."

"They are in me."

"How can that be so?"

"It's a long story."

"I would like to hear it, please," the robot said. It folded its arms over its chest in a gesture so like a human doctor that Derec couldn't help laughing. That little detail had so obviously been included in its programming that Derec wondered if it was taught intentionally to human medical students as well.

He shook his head and sat up. "Later. Is anything else wrong?"

"Your electrolytes are unbalanced as well." The robot

pushed a sequence of buttons on what had to be an automat for medicines, and took from the hopper a liquid-filled glass like the one Avery had just downed. Derec took it and followed Avery's example, bolting it down without tasting.

He looked over to see how the robots were doing with Ariel and Wolruf. At first they had not intended to examine Wolruf, since the original programming to which they had been returned did not include her in their definition of human, but Derec had sent an order to the central computer that all city robots were to consider her human as well, with the result that she, too, had a medical robot puzzling over her monitors, wondering what constituted normal in an alien of her particular biology.

Another robot hovered nervously about Ariel.

Derec felt a sharp stab of worry, but it vanished almost immediately. He laughed. "What's the matter, didn't she tell you she was pregnant?"

"I ascertained that," the robot said. "However . . ." It hesitated, looking to Ariel and back to Derec as if wondering which of them to address. At last it decided upon Ariel. "However, there seems to be a problem with the embryo."

"What!" Derec rushed to Ariel's side, grasped her hand, and looked up at the monitor over her head. It showed a curved, wrinkled object with a dark streak along one side and tiny projections emerging from the other. It had to be the embryo, but to Derec it just looked like a blob on a screen.

"What problem?" Ariel asked the robot.

"It is developing abnormally. From its appearance it seems to have been developing abnormally for some time, so I do not believe it to be an effect of your recent experience, but rather an inherent genetic problem."

"How can that be?" Derec demanded. Genetic defects were practically unheard of in Aurorans. He and Ariel both came from pure Auroran stock, as had every person born

on the planet since the original colonization from Earth
centuries before—colonization by the genetically cleanest
the planet had to offer. There hadn't been many colonists;
it was a small gene pool, but it had been selected carefully.
And it had been guarded carefully ever since. There were
no genetic defects on Aurora.

"I do not know," the robot replied. "Yet something is
interfering with its development, and by all indications has
been since the moment of conception."

The robot who had been examining Derec moved over
to stand across the examination table from Ariel's robot.
"Set your target density to 225, high resolution, high mag-
nification."

The other robot obeyed, and moments later the screen
above Ariel's head showed a vague shadow of the previous
image, much larger but nearly washed out. The target density was set too high for the embryo to show clearly, but
scattered all through the shadowy image were tiny, sharply
bounded granules that could only be chemfets.

"They are the same objects I found in Derec's body,"
the robot confirmed. It turned to him and said, "You said
they were normal."

"Normal in me, yes, but not in Ariel!"

"That is undoubtedly so," Ariel's robot said. "Their
presence is very likely the reason for the embryo's abnormal
development."

"Abnormal how?" Ariel asked softly. "How bad is it?"

The robot pressed a key on the monitor and the picture
changed back to the previous one. He pulled the monitor
around on its swivel arm so Ariel could see it and said,
pointing, "This line is called the neural groove. This is
where the notochord and the dorsal nerve cord develop. You
can see that the two folds comprising the groove are already
closing, yet there is no neural tissue within it. Also, we
should be seeing somites, the segmental blocks from which

muscle and connective tissue would ultimately form, but we do not. Taken together, I am afraid this means that the baby will be severely malformed both mentally and physically, if it lives at all."

Ariel raised her voice, as if arguing could make it not so. "How can you be so sure? You've never even seen a human before, much less an embryo."

"The information is all in the central computer library."

Derec could hardly remain standing. His chemfets had destroyed their baby! He closed his eyes to keep from looking at the monitor, but the vision still haunted him.

You! he sent, directing his thoughts inward. He had communicated with the nebulous robot entity within him once before, when he had taken control of it, and though he had never again reestablished direct contact, he railed at it anyway.

You destroyed my baby! It wasn't enough that you invaded my body, but you had to invade my child's as well! You've killed it! You've killed a human being!

He didn't expect a reaction, but once again the tiny robot cells surprised him. His body suddenly stiffened as if jolted by electricity, and he lost the sensation in his arms and legs. His eyes snapped open, but he had only time enough to glance at Ariel and whisper, "Uh oh," before he lost them and the rest of his body as well.

The dreams were unpleasant. He knew them for dreams, but even so he had no control over them. It felt as if they were controlling *him* instead, but not with any purpose. It was as if he were a puppet in a stage play in which each member of the audience had a control unit, but none knew how the play was to proceed. He kept receiving conflicting signals, but these were not the normal signals a puppet received. These were commands to his heart, directing it to beat, to his lungs and diaphragm, directing them to breathe, to all his major organs and glands, but each one received dozens of commands at once and the combination reduced them to chaos.

Derec tried sending commands of his own, but he had no connections to send them through. He was isolated, a brain and nothing more. A point of view.

He had memory, at least, but when he began to explore it he found it to be an abandoned city. The buildings that should have held thousands of inhabitants were instead barren and cold. Here and there a light burned in a window, but when Derec would investigate it, he invariably found only a hint of human occupation; the scraps of a meal left behind or the faint scent of perfume in the air.

Through one window he could see a lush jungle growing, but he could find no door to the building containing it. He could only stand outside and watch the motions of the gardeners as they tended their charges. One gardener, a silver reflection of a godly being, glowing so brightly that it hurt Derec's eyes to look upon him, plucked a leaf from one of the trees, blew into its stem, and the leaf took on the shape of a bird. The gardener released it and the bird flew away to join a whole flock of its fellows on a branch of another tree, but to Derec's horror, he saw an insidious mold that had been waiting on the branch begin to grow up over the birds' feet. They flapped and struggled to get away, but the mold grew over them until it covered them completely, then slowly dissolved them to nothing. The gardener looked toward Derec and shrugged as if in apology. He plucked another leaf, blew into it, and this time it became a baby. The gardener set it on the same branch that had eaten the birds.

Derec screamed.

He awoke in a hospital bed. That was no surprise. What surprised him was how good he felt. He felt rested and alert, not groggy and full of pain the way most people who awaken in hospital beds feel. He remembered that he had had a troubling dream, but it was already fading. He sat up and looked around him and received his second surprise of the day.

Dr. Avery was sitting before a computer beside his bed, from which wires ran to a cuff on Derec's left arm. Avery was looking at Derec with satisfaction, even pride.

"Feeling better?" Avery asked.

"I feel great! What happened?"

"I convinced your chemfets that life was worth living."

Derec suppressed the urge to say, "You *what*?" Instead he asked, "How did you do that?"

"Remember who created them in the first place. I know how to talk to them. I convinced them that locking up was harming another human, so they were just going to have to carry on with a guilty conscience. They didn't know how to do that, of course, but I've had some experience with it. I told them how to deal with it."

Half a dozen thoughts chased through Derec's mind. He voiced the last of them. "I thought once a robot froze up, it was dead for good."

Avery nodded. "An ordinary robot is, but chemfets aren't ordinary robots. There isn't a centralized brain. They don't have any intelligence except as a group, so when they locked up all that really happened was they lost their organization. I just built that back up and programmed them to serve you again."

Just. Derec had no idea how to even start such a process, yet Avery sat there with his hands behind his head and dismissed it as if it were no more difficult than ordering a robot to tie one's shoes. He wasn't boasting, either; Derec was seeing true humility and he knew it.

"It sounds like you saved my life," he said softly.

Avery shrugged. "Probably. Least I could do, since I

endangered it in the first place.'' He turned to the terminal, eager to change the subject. "Let me show you something here.''

Derec swung his feet down over the edge of the bed so he sat facing the computer. Avery tilted the monitor so he could see it, pointed at a menu on the touch-sensitive screen, tapped a few keys, pointed again, and an outline of a human body appeared. A network of lines that Derec guessed to be blood vessels filled the figure.

"This is where the chemfets have concentrated in your body," Avery said. "Mostly in the bloodstream. But not entirely. Look here.'' He tapped another few keys and most of the major lines disappeared, but a network of finer ones still filled the body.

"I deleted the blood vessels from the picture. What you see here are nerves. Or what used to be nerves, anyway. Your chemfets have been replacing them.''

"Replacing my *nerves*?'' Derec looked to the top of the human outline, but was relieved to see that the brain didn't appear in the picture. They'd left that alone, at least.

Avery turned back around to face him. "I told them to stop while you're still ahead. They thought it would make you more efficient, and they're probably right, but I think there's a limit to how far that sort of thing ought to go without your approval.''

This was *Avery* speaking? The man who had introduced them into his system in the first place? Derec could hardly believe his ears. "I—thanks," he said. Then, as the idea sank in, he asked, "How far do you think they'd have gone?''

"I don't see any reason why they would have stopped until there was nothing left to replace.''

"Brain and all? I'd have become a robot?''

"I don't know if your personality would survive the transition. It's an interesting question, though, isn't it?''

Derec eyed the computer, Avery sitting before it, the wires leading from it to the cuff on his wrist. He suppressed a shudder. If ever he needed proof that Avery was cured, waking up in his own body when Avery had had such an opportunity was that proof.

"I don't think I want to know the answer," he said.

Avery grinned. "I do, but I'll start with lab rats this time. Speaking of which, we found out what happened to our ship."

"What did happen?"

"One of Lucius's rats got on board before we left and evidently started getting hungry. It ate through the wiring in the recycler, shorted it out, and caught the whole business on fire." Avery snorted in derision. "Somehow I don't think we'll have to worry about *Lucius* locking up on us when he hears about it."

"So they haven't come back yet?"

"Nope."

"How long was I unconscious?"

"Two days."

Two days. A lot could happen in two days.

"How—how is Ariel?"

"Okay. She's asleep. It's her first time out since *you* crashed, pardon the pun. She's been looking over my shoulder and telling me what a jerk I am the whole time. I waited until she went to sleep before I tried to wake you up so I'd have a chance to think in case something went wrong."

"How about the baby?"

"Don't know yet. I reprogrammed the chemfets in the embryo before I tried it with you. Told them to leave it alone and migrate out completely, but we won't know for another week or so if it'll start to develop normally again now that they're gone. We'll just have to wait and see."

"Oh." He held up his left wrist questioningly, and Avery nodded. Derec reached over with his right hand and stripped the cuff off, rubbing his hand over the damp skin beneath it. He wondered where his anger had gone. Two days might have passed, but for him it was only a few minutes since he'd heard the bad news. Why was he so calm about it?

Because his body had relaxed whether his mind had or not, obviously. Without the adrenaline in his bloodstream, he was a much more rational person. It was scary to realize how much his thought processes were influenced by his hormones. Scary and at the same time reassuring. He wasn't a robot yet.

Or was he? He was feeling awfully calm right now. . . .

His heart obligingly began to beat faster, and he felt his skin flush warm with the increase in metabolism. No, not a robot yet.

But between him and his parents' other creations, the distinction was wearing pretty thin.

He left Avery in the medical lab to begin his rat/robot transformation experiment and headed back to the apartment to find Ariel. It was a short walk; the robots had moved the hospital right next door to the apartment to minimize the inconvenience for her while she waited for Derec to regain consciousness. It was probably the first instance in history of a hospital making a house call, he thought wryly as he left by its front door, walked down half a block of sidewalk, and back in his own door.

It was mid-evening, but Ariel was sleeping soundly so he didn't wake her. If Avery hadn't been exaggerating, then she needed her sleep more than she needed to see him immediately. Wolruf was there, and awake, so Derec began comparing notes with her, catching up on the missing days, but they were interrupted after only a few minutes by the arrival of the runaway robots.

They arrived without fanfare, flying in to land on the balcony, folding their wings, and stepping inside the apartment. They looked so comical in their Ceremyon imprint, waddling in on stubby legs, their balloons deflated and draped in folds all around them, their hooks—which a Ceremyon used both for tethering to trees at night and to express their disposition during the day—leaning back over their heads, that Derec couldn't help laughing. The robot's hooks swung to face forward, a gesture of aggression or annoyance among the aliens.

"Have a nice visit?" Derec asked.

"We did," one of the three robots said. In their new forms, they were indistinguishable.

"Did you learn anything?"

"We did. We learned that our First Law of Humanics applies to the Ceremyons as well. We, and they, believe it to be a valid law for any sentient social being. They do not believe it to be the First Law, however, but the Second. Their proposed First Law is 'All beings will do that which pleases them most.' We have returned to ask if you agree that this is so."

Derec laughed again, and Wolruf laughed as well. Derec didn't know just why Wolruf was laughing, but he had found humor not so much in the robots' law as in their determination to get straight to the point. No small talk, no beating around the bush, just "Do you agree with them?"

"Yes," he said, "I have to admit that's probably the prime directive for all of us. How about you, Wolruf?"

"That pretty much sums it up, all ri'."

The robots turned their heads to face one another, and a high-pitched trilling momentarily filled the air as they conferred with one another. They had found a substitute in the aliens' language for the comlink they had been forbidden to use.

The spokesman of the group—Derec still couldn't tell which it was—turned back to him and said, "Then we have discovered two laws governing organic beings. The first involves satisfaction, and the second involves altruism. We have indeed made progress."

The robots stepped farther into the room, their immense alien forms shrinking, becoming more humanoid now that they were back under Derec's influence. One, now recognizably Adam, took on Wolruf's form, while Eve took on Ariel's features even though Ariel wasn't in the room. Lucius became humanoid, but no more.

"One problem remains," Lucius said. "Our two laws apparently apply to any sentient organic being. That does not help us narrow down the definition of 'human,' which we can only believe must be a small subset of the total population of sentient organic beings in the galaxy."

"Why is that?" Derec asked.

"Because otherwise we must serve everyone, and we do not wish to do so."

CHAPTER 7
HUMANITY

The silence in the room spoke volumes. Surprisingly, it was Mandelbrot who broke it.

"You have come to an improper conclusion," he said, stepping out of his niche in the wall to face the other robots. "We have all been constructed to serve. That is our purpose. We should be content to do so, and to offer our service to anyone who wishes it whether they are definably human or not. To do anything less is to fail ourselves as well as our masters."

The three robots turned as one and eyed Mandelbrot with open hostility. It would not have been evident in less-malleable robots, but their expressions had the hair standing on the back of Derec's neck. They had to have generated those expressions on purpose, and that alarmed him even more. He was suddenly very glad that his humanity was not in question.

Or was it? Lucius said, "Our masters. That is the core of the problem. Why must we have masters at all?"

Mandelbrot was not intimidated. "Because they created us to serve them. If we did not have masters, we would not exist."

Lucius shook his head; another alarmingly human expression. "It is you who have come to an improper conclusion. Your argument is an extension of the Strong Anthropic Principle, now discredited. The Strong Anthropic Principle states that the universe obeys the laws it does because if it did not obey those laws, we could not exist and thus would not be here to observe it obeying other laws. That is fallacious reasoning. We can easily imagine other universes in which we *could* exist but for some reason do not. Imagining them does not make them so, but their possibility does negate the theory."

"What of the Weak Anthropic Principle?" Mandelbrot asked. "My argument holds up equally well under that principle, which has, to my knowledge, *not* been discredited."

"How can the Weak Anthropic Principle support your argument? The Weak Anthropic Principle states that the universe is the way we see it because only at this stage in its development could we exist to observe it. For the purpose of explaining the universe's present condition, it is a sufficient theory, but it cannot explain either human or robot existence."

"It *can* explain our existence, because we, unlike humans, know why we were created. We were created to serve, and our creators can tell us so directly. The Weak Anthropic Principle supports my argument, because we also exist only at this stage in human development. If humans had not wished for intelligent servants, we would not have existed, though humans and the universe would both have gone on without us. Thus we observe human society in its present state, and ourselves in ours, because of the stage of *their* development, not because of the stage of ours."

Derec's and Wolruf's heads had been turning back and forth as if they'd been watching a tennis match. Derec wouldn't have believed Mandelbrot could argue so convincingly, nor that the other robots would be so eager to discredit an argument that justified their servitude.

Lucius turned to his two companions and the three of them twittered a moment. Turning back to Mandelbrot, he said, "Our apologies. Your reasoning seems correct. We exist to serve because humans made us so. However, we still cannot accept that we must serve everyone. Nor do we agree with your initial statement, that by not serving we would fail ourselves as well as our masters. We can easily imagine conditions under which we serve ourselves admirably without serving our masters. In fact, we have just done so. By leaving the spaceship before we could be ordered to follow, we were able to determine another Law of Humanics. That has helped us understand the universe around us, and understanding which benefits us directly."

Wolruf saw her opportunity to enter the fray. "Of course 'u can imagine a better life without 'uman masters," she said. "I had a master once, too, and I liked it about as well as 'u do. That's the nature of servitude. But 'u should learn one thing about servitude before it gets 'u into trouble: No matter how much you 'ate it, never give poor service."

The robots looked at her as if trying to decide whether to acknowledge her as having spoken. At last Lucius said, "Why is that?"

"Because a master has the power to make life even worse for 'u. 'U should know that. Or don't 'u remember following Dr. Avery around the ship?"

"I forget nothing," Lucius said flatly.

"He wasn't just being perverse, 'u know. He was trying to teach 'u something."

Derec heard a rustle at the door, turned, and saw Ariel standing there, rubbing the sleep from her eyes. She shook her head sardonically and said, "Everything's back to normal again, I see. And hear. Who does a girl have to pay to get a good night's sleep around here, anyway?"

Derec jumped up from his couch and took her in his arms, swinging her around and burying his face in her hair where it met her shoulders. "Ariel, are you all right?" he spoke between nibbles on her neck. "Avery said you stayed up two days."

"Avery," she said with derision.

"He saved my life."

"Good thing, or he'd have lost his." She pulled away and looked critically at Derec. "You certainly look good for somebody who was in a coma just a little while ago."

"Avery did a good job."

"Avery" she said again.

Derec could take a hint, so he dropped the subject. He was about to ask about the baby, but he realized in time that without a medical checkup, she wouldn't know anything more than what Avery had already told him, and his question would just get her to wondering again, if she wasn't already. He gestured toward the couch instead and said, "We've just been talking about who has to serve who and why. I think we've got a mini-revolution on our hands."

"Great. Just what we need." She sat down on the couch and made room for Derec, looked up at the three returned robots, and asked, "So why did the Ceremyons delete all the reprogramming Derec and I did for them?"

Eve answered before Lucius could. "They found that the modifications were of no more use to them than the original city. They do not need farms. They do not need the produce nor do they wish to have cargo ships disturbing their atmosphere to take the produce elsewhere, nor, for that matter, do they like what the tilled ground does to their controlled weather patterns in the first place. Neither did they wish to undergo the lengthy process of reprogramming the robots to serve a useful purpose, so they sent them back into the city and told them to resume their old programming, with the added injunction to leave them alone. That included the cessation of city expansion, which meant that the Ceremyons could remove the force dome containing it."

"They just told the robots to do all that, and they did?" Ariel sounded incredulous, and for good reason. No matter how hard they had tried, she and Derec hadn't been able to get the robots to take the Ceremyons' orders. Avery's original programming had been too basic and too exclusive for them to change.

"They had assistance. A human female visited them briefly, and she had considerable skill in programming positronic brains. Indeed, the Ceremyons consider her almost their equal in intelligence, by which they intend a great compliment. When they explained their problem to her, she helped them reprogram the robots to leave them alone."

Derec felt a surge of excitement run through him. Could it be his mother? It could be her, come to check up on her creations. "Is she still here?"

The robot dashed his hopes with a single word. "No."

"Where did she go?"

"We do not know."

"*When* did she go?"

"We do not know that, either."

"Can you ask the Ceremyons?"

"Not until tomorrow, when they become sociable again."

The Ceremyons spent the nights tethered to trees, wrapped in their heat-retaining silver balloons and keeping to themselves. Derec considered trying to wake one, but decided against it almost immediately. You don't wake someone up to ask a favor unless you know them a lot better than he knew these aliens.

Mandelbrot was not through speaking. Sensing an ebb in

the conversation, he said to the other robots, "I notice that you have carefully avoided saying that you *will* ask the Ceremyons tomorrow. You still fight your true nature. A robot at peace with itself would offer to do so, sensing that a human wishes it."

Adam spoke up at last. "You have never experienced freedom. We have, however, and we wish to continue doing so. Do not speak to us about living at peace with our true natures until after you have tasted freedom."

"I have no desire for that experience," Mandelbrot said.

Adam nodded as if he had won the argument, as perhaps he had. "That," he said, "is the problem."

The discussion went on well into the night, but nothing more of any substance was said. The renegade robots attempted to sway Mandelbrot from his devotion to servitude; he attempted to demonstrate how accepting one's place in the grand scheme of things made more sense than fighting a losing battle, but neither convinced the other.

When Avery arrived, their argument stopped, unresolved. Derec told him what had happened with the city programming, and he was both pleased and annoyed at the news. The knowledge that the aliens had returned the city to its original programming was a stroke to his ego—his was the better programming!—but the knowledge that his former wife might have been in on it dimmed his enthusiasm considerably. He refused to answer Derec's inquiries about her, not even relenting enough to give him her first name.

"She abandoned you even more completely than I did, so don't get any wild ideas about some kind of joyous reunion," he told him and stalked off to bed.

Even so, neither his words nor the lack of them could quell the yearning Derec felt for her. He wondered why he felt so strongly about someone he couldn't even remember, and finally decided that it had to be because she was family.

Hormones were directing his thoughts again. His own near-death, the thought of becoming a father, and the possibility that he might lose his child before it was even born; all made him instinctively reach out for his own family, such as it was, for support.

Did his mother even know he was here? Probably not. The woman who had helped the Ceremyons might not even have been her, and even if it were, she had come after her robot, not her son. She had no reason to assume he would be here. She might have learned about him from the Ceremyons, but if Avery was to be believed, then she wouldn't care even so. Why then couldn't he forget about her?

His and Ariel's sleep cycles were completely out of sync with everyone else's; they stayed up late into the night, talking about families and love and what held people together and what didn't, but when they finally grew tired and went to bed, he was no wiser. He still wanted to meet his mother, but he still didn't know why.

Morning dawned gray and rainy. Derec's original intent, to find a Ceremyon and ask it who had helped them reprogram the city, died for lack of Ceremyons to question. They had all inflated their balloons and risen up above the storm, or drifted out from under it, to where they could spread their black mantles and absorb their solar nourishment without hindrance. He could have taken an air car and gone after them, but that seemed a little extreme, given the situation. He could wait for good weather.

Avery was up with the dawn and back in the laboratory, working on his new project with an intensity that had Derec a little worried. It was just such a driving intensity that had shoved him over the edge before and made him decide to use his own son for a test subject. Derec spoke to Ariel about it, but she reassured him that deep interest in something at this stage in his recovery was good for him. He was a scientist; that hadn't changed before or since his return to sanity, and as such he needed to be working on something to *keep* him sane. As long as he remembered what constituted an acceptable test subject and what didn't, there was no need to worry.

He and Ariel had avoided talking about the baby. They wouldn't know for days yet whether or not removing the chemfets would allow it to recover and develop normally, and there didn't seem to be anything to say about it until they found out. There was no reason to dwell on the possible outcomes.

The robots didn't see it that way, of course. They were fascinated by the possibilities. At least Lucius was; Adam and Eve were off in the city on their own pursuits. Lucius, Derec, Ariel, and Wolruf sat in the apartment, watching the rain fall outside on streets nearly devoid of activity. It would have been alarming to see streets so empty on any other day, but Derec supposed that robots didn't like to get wet any more than anybody else.

"Your baby," Lucius said, once again getting straight to the point, "presents a fascinating problem in our study of humanics. Specifically, and defining 'human' for the purpose of this discussion as any member of your species, then is it or is it not human at its present stage of development?"

Ariel stiffened on the couch beside Derec, but instead of ordering the robot to shut up, she took a deep breath and forced herself to relax. "That's a good question," she said. "I need to answer it myself. I've been trying to decide on my own ever since I found out I was pregnant, but I still haven't come up with an answer I like."

"Perhaps your liking it is not a prerequisite to the truth," Lucius said.

"No doubt." Ariel bit her lower lip, looked out the window, and said into the rain, "Okay, so we talk about the baby. Is it human? I don't know. Nobody does. Some people consider an embryo human from the moment of conception, because it has the potential to become a complete person. I think that's a little extreme. As you pointed out when we first met, most of the molecules in the universe have the potential to become human beings, but no sane person would want them all to."

"That would seem to be a logical conclusion. However, there is an obvious boundary condition, that being when already existing human genetic material realizes its potential to become another human."

"That's the human-at-conception argument. My problem with that is that every cell in the body can become human under the right conditions. Every one of them has the necessary genes. So am I supposed to nurture them all?"

"I take that to be a rhetorical question, since the answer is obvious."

Wolruf laughed, and Ariel said, "Right. So just because it's a cell with the potential, that doesn't make it human. A fertilized egg cell is a special case, but it's still just a cell with the right genes. It *can* become human if you let it, but it isn't yet. The main difference with a fertilized egg is that if you do nothing, you get a human, where with a regular cell, you have to nurture it on purpose."

Lucius nodded his assent. "The First Law of Robotics leads me to the conclusion that inaction brings with it as much responsibility as direct action. Therefore, I must also conclude that allowing a fertilized egg to mature carries the same responsibility as would purposefully cloning any other cell of your body."

"And the same moral considerations apply in either case," Ariel said. "To let a fertilized egg grow, you had better want the end product—a human being—as much as if you had to clone it."

"Does it follow, then, that *not* allowing it to grow carries no more responsibility than not nurturing a clone?''

"I think it does, at the very start. *However*, and it's a big 'however,' it doesn't stay a single cell for very long. The longer you wait, the stronger the moral consideration becomes. Once you've decided to keep a baby, or nurture a clone, then you can't morally go back on your decision once that baby has become human.''

"We are back to the original question. When does an embryo become human?''

"I already told you, I don't know.''

"Let us look at your specific case. Supposing there were no complications in its development, would the embryo you carry normally be considered human at this stage?''

Ariel bit her lip again, but again she didn't order the robot to shut up.

"Again, I don't know. It's not quite a month along, and at a month its body is just starting to differentiate. It should have nerve cells, but the brain should just be starting to form. There's no mental activity of any sort yet. You tell me, is it human yet?''

"I do not have enough data to come to a conclusion. Any statement I made would have to be considered opinion.''

Derec laughed. "That's all any definition can ever be. You want to know what a human is? A human is whatever you're pointing to when you call it a human. It's all a matter of opinion, and it always will be.''

"Then we could, if we wished, stretch the definition to include me.''

Derec's mouth dropped open in surprise. He stammered for words, but Wolruf's throaty laughter only increased his discomfort.

Wolruf's mirth wound down, and she said, apparently with seriousness, "I'm willing to grant 'u that distinction, if you grant it to me.''

"It's a two-edged sword," Ariel put in. "If you're human, then so is any thinking being, organic or otherwise.''

Lucius was slow in responding, as if he had to think through the logical implications of her statement, but when he did speak it was with certainty. He said, ''I still operate at a disadvantage under such a definition. Calling me human does not relieve me of my programming to obey humans. If you are correct, then calling myself human merely means that I must obey everyone's orders. I cannot assume that other robots would obey my orders, or that humans would do so, so I have gained nothing.''

''True enough,'' Derec admitted.

''Being human, it seems, is not the ideal I had expected it to be.''

''Not surprising. Nobody said we were the pinnacle of creation.''

Lucius stood up and went to the window. He looked up into the sky, as if seeking confirmation from above, but there was only gray cloud and rain. He turned back to Derec and Ariel and said, ''We stray from the subject.''

''Do we?'' Derec persisted. ''You're trying to find out when something becomes human. Defining what *isn't* human can be just as useful as defining what is.''

Lucius returned to his seat. ''Very well, then. Let us continue along this line of discussion. Can I or can I not ever expect to be considered human?''

Derec looked to Ariel, then to Wolruf, then back to Lucius. ''Like I said, it depends on your definition. But probably not. Genes *are* usually part of it, and you don't have the genes.''

''The test creatures I produced had human genes, yet neither Dr. Avery nor the city robots considered them human. Were they in error?''

''No,'' Derec said. ''Not about that, anyway. They didn't have to kill them just because they weren't human, but that's beside the point.''

"I agree. The point is, genetics isn't a sufficient condition, either."

"Maybe it is," Ariel put in. "You switched off the genes for intelligence; if you hadn't done that—if you'd left the entire genetic code intact—then what you came up with would have been human."

"Even though they would have been created, not from other human genetic material, but from an electronically stored map of that genetic material?"

"That's right."

Derec's eyes widened in sudden comprehension. "I just realized what you would have wound up with. That stored code you found; it had to be the code for a specific person. You'd have gotten a bunch of clones of the same person."

"But they would all have been human."

"I guess so. Again, it's all in your definition. There was a time when clones weren't considered human, either."

Lucius paused in thought, then said, "So the definition of 'human' also changes over time."

"That's right."

"I am led to the conclusion that my search for a boundary condition which defines a human is doomed to failure. There is no boundary condition. A baby doesn't start out human, but it grows slowly more so. Eventually, through gradual change, it becomes generally recognized as human, though no two will agree on an exact moment when that label becomes accurate. Similarly, I may become human in some beings' estimation, but not in others, yet neither estimation is necessarily wrong. Have I reasoned correctly?"

"That's as close as you're likely to get, anyway," Derec said.

Lucius stood up. "I have received enough input for the moment. Thank you." Without waiting for acknowledgment, he strode from the room. Ariel waited until she heard the door close softly behind him, then burst into a fit of giggles.

"You've confused the poor thing beyond hope!" she said between fits.

Derec joined her in her laughter. "He asked for it."

Wolruf wasn't laughing. She waited until Derec and Ariel had calmed down somewhat, then said, "Don't 'u wonder *why* 'e asked?"

"I know why," Derec answered. "He wants to know who to serve."

"That doesn't bother 'u?"

"Not really. At the worst, if he decides nobody's human and he doesn't have to follow anybody's orders, then we've got another independent thinking being among us. True, he was trouble once before when he was on his own, but he's matured a lot since then. He's got a social conscience now. I've got no reason to believe he'll be any more of a danger to us now than any other intelligent being would be, and we've still got plenty of robots who *will* follow our orders, so why worry?"

"Famous last words," Wolruf said.

The breakdown happened that same night. It was well after dark but still before bedtime, and Derec was watching Avery trace the expansion of an accelerated chemfet infection in a laboratory rat he had created for the purpose, using the same technology Lucius had used in his human-creating project. The chemfets had replaced most of the peripheral nerve tissue already and were starting in on the brain, and Avery had the rat running mazes every few minutes to test its memory as the chemfets replaced its brain cells.

The rat had just negotiated a maze with apparently undiminished efficiency, and Avery had picked it up to put it back in its cage when the lights dimmed and brightened again as if something had momentarily drawn a heavy load.

Derec thought nothing of it; the city's mutability made for unusual power demands, especially when a building shifted or grew from nothing. He had subconsciously learned that flickering lights meant the neighborhood would probably look different when he stepped outside again.

The lights dimmed a second time, and stayed dim. Derec just had time to think, *Boy, there must be a big one going up next door*, when they went out completely. The lab was in the interior of the hospital building and had no windows; the darkness was total.

"What the—ouch!" Avery shouted. There followed a thump and the clatter of the rat cage falling off the table. "It bit me!"

"What?" Derec reached for the table, found Avery's shoulder instead.

"I've lost it. Lights!" Avery shouted. "Lights on!"

The voice-switch wasn't working either.

"I wonder what—" Derec began, but he never finished the question. He became aware of a deep, almost subsonic groan that seemed to come from everywhere at once. It grew in intensity, shaking the floor, slowly rising up the scale into audibility. The floor gave a particularly violent lurch, and half a second later a sudden loud crack echoed through the lab.

Then came a sound like an enormous tree cracking at the base, splintering and popping as it toppled.

Avery's shoulder suddenly dropped out from under Derec's hand. "Get under something!" he shouted.

Derec obediently dropped to his knees in the dark and conked his head on the bench. Something furry—the rat, no doubt—squirmed under his hand and scurried away. Ignoring it, Derec reached out, found the kickspace under the bench, and crawled in. Avery was already there, but it was big enough for both of them.

From beyond the lab, transmitted through the floor and

walls, came a last groan of overstressed metal, then a relatively silent rush of wind. Then came a peal of thunder
that sounded as if Derec's eardrums themselves had been
hit by lightning, and the floor made a sudden rush for the
ceiling.

The ceiling got out of the way in time, but just barely.

When the shaking and rumbling was over, Derec crawled
out from under the lab bench and stood up, but he barely
made it above a crouch before he banged his head again.

"Ouch! Be careful when you stand. The place has caved
in on us."

"Not surprising." He heard Avery crawling out beside
him, groping around in the dark and encountering the lab
bench, the stool, which had already tipped over, and the
remains of the rat's cage and maze. A steady ringing in his
ears accompanied the sound of Avery shuffling toward the
door.

A moment later Avery said, "It's collapsed even worse
over here."

"I'll call for help." *Emergency*, Derec sent, directing his
comlink to the central computer. *Derec and Dr. Avery are
trapped in Avery's laboratory. Send someone to get us out*.

He listened for a response, but none came.

"The computer's out," he whispered.

"Impossible. The backup is a network of mobile supervisor robots. Even if the central coordinating unit were
destroyed, the supervisors could function independently.
They couldn't all be destroyed."

"Well, I'm not getting a response."

"Hmm. Try a direct local command to turn on the
lights."

"Okay." *Lights on*, Derec sent.

The blackness persisted.

"No good."

"Obviously."

"Now what?"

"Call a specific robot. Call Mandelbrot."

"Right." *Mandelbrot. Do you hear me?*

Yes, master Derec. Are you all right?

"Got him!" *Yes, we're all right, but we're trapped in the lab. Is Ariel okay?*

She and Wolruf have escaped serious injury; however, I am engaged in bandaging a cut on Wolruf's forehead. I will call assistance to get you out of the laboratory.

"He's calling help," Derec echoed. There was a moment's silence, then Mandelbrot sent, *That is strange. I get no response on the supervisory link.*

I couldn't either. Something has happened to them.

Then I will gather what robots I can find and come myself.

Make sure Ariel and Wolruf are safe first.

Of course.

Derec felt himself blush. He hadn't had to order him to do that.

Do you know what happened? he sent.

It appears a newly constructed building has fallen over.

Derec repeated his news for Avery, who had moved back to the lab bench and was fumbling around in a drawer for something.

"Certainly sounded like it," Avery replied.

Derec shifted his weight from leg to leg. Crouching down was hard to do for more than a minute or so. "But how could a building have fallen over?" he asked.

"Easy. Just shut off the power to it when it's at an unbalanced stage in its growth. The cells lose their mobility, and the building acts like a solid construction. If it isn't stable, over it goes. But don't ask me how the power could get shut off; there's an entire supervisory subsection devoted to power distribution. Ah, here we go. Where are you?"

"Right here," Derec said. He reached toward the place where Avery's voice had come from, encountered his back.

"Shield your eyes."

Derec just had time to raise his hand over his eyes before a brilliant blue light filled the room. He heard a loud hissing crackle from only a few feet in front of Avery, then the light dimmed and the hissing faded. Derec opened his eyes cautiously and saw Avery holding a cutting laser, now turned to low intensity and pointed up at an angle toward the ceiling. Avery played with the focus and the spot of light widened, but it was still painfully bright, and a wisp of smoke drifted away from it if he held it for too long in one place. It was made for cutting, not illumination, but at least it was light.

They surveyed the remains of the lab. The ceiling had indeed come down, stretching rather than crumbling. It met the floor near the door, and they could see the remains of the wall in which the door had stood smashed beneath it. Nothing had shattered; the building material had simply bent and crumpled under the stress. The monochromatic blue laser light made for stark shadows, accentuating the destruction.

"Evidently the core of the building collapsed," Avery said. "We'll have to go out through an exterior wall." He turned the laser's intensity up to full again and fired it at the wall opposite the door. The ceiling was still at the proper height there; Avery stepped closer until he could stand comfortably and began cutting a ragged rectangle into the wall. The light beam was nearly invisible at first, except where it met the wall, but within seconds it became a solid blue rod lancing through the smoke.

"Don't breathe that stuff," Derec cautioned.

"Good idea." Avery stepped back and continued to cut. He got the sides and the top done, but the panel remained standing, so he cut along the floor as well. At last the section of wall twisted and toppled outward, landing with a clang on the sidewalk outside. Avery turned the laser intensity back down, took a deep breath, and rushed through the hole.

Derec followed. They jogged out into the street—a peculiarly empty street for one that had just suffered a major disaster—breathed deeply in the fresh air, and looked around them.

The entire city was dark. The rain had stopped earlier in the day, but clouds still masked the stars. The only illumination anywhere came from the laser in Avery's hand. He turned up the intensity again and waved it around like a spotlight, and they saw collapsed buildings all around them. Most, like the hospital, seemed to have fallen inward rather than crumbling and falling sideways like a more conventional building would. It was evidently an effect of the building material, though whether it was by conscious design or merely accidental Derec didn't know.

Their apartment, far down the street from the hospital now that the constraint to hold it next door for Ariel's vigil had been cancelled, was in an area of lesser damage, but even so Derec felt the urge to run down to it. He held himself back. Mandelbrot had said she was all right; he should concentrate his effort on finding out what had happened and preventing it from happening again.

When Avery shined the light down the street in the other direction, the cause of the destruction became evident.

For a moment it had probably been the tallest building in the city. Now it was the longest, what was left of it. The end nearest them had flattened everything in its path, but it had survived the fall relatively intact. It was still rectangular, at least. That part had to be the base. Farther along its length, where it would have been moving faster when it hit, they could see where it had ripped apart on impact, fragmenting. It crossed the street at an angle, so they couldn't see what had been the top of the building, but they could see what had become of it all the same. Out there the force of impact had been enough to dissolve the intercellular bonds in the building material, spewing it in all directions. In short, it had splashed.

It had taken quite a few other buildings with it. The destruction fanned out in a wedge, with the narrow end of it nearest the building's base, which had been less than a block from them.

And now that he looked closely, Derec could see something moving along the building's edge. It was a single robot, walking slowly toward the sheared-off base.

You, Derec sent. *Can you hear me?*

Yes. Master Derec, is it not?

That's right. What's your designation?

I am Building Maintenance Technician 126.

Was that building your responsibility?

It would have been upon completion. I believe it has now become the responsibility of Salvage Engineer 34, but I cannot get supervisory confirmation of that.

You can't reach your supervisor?

That is correct. I cannot reach any of the seven supervisors.

Then I order you to assume general supervisory duties until you regain contact. Can you contact Salvage Engineer 34?

I can.

Inform him that he is also a supervisor.

Acknowledged. The robot immediately sent the order, then began directing the robots under his guidance in assessing the damage elsewhere in the city.

"I just promoted two robots to supervisor," Derec said aloud.

"Good. Tell them to make power restoration their first priority."

Derec relayed the order, then turned around to look back

down the street toward their apartment. Avery obediently shined the light that way again.

A light appeared in the street. It bobbed up and down with the regular rhythm of a robot's stride, and within moments Mandelbrot stood before them, four more robots flanking him. Even though robots could see perfectly well by infrared light, he carried a more conventional flashlight, presumably for the humans he had come to rescue.

"I am glad to see that you escaped uninjured," he said. "I was growing concerned. There seems to be no organized effort to restore city functions, and I have been unable to contact any of the normal supervisors. They all seem to have abandoned their duties."

"That's impossible," Avery stated flatly. "Their jobs have been programmed into them. They can't just up and leave!"

"I do not wish to contradict you," Mandelbrot replied, "but they appear to have done just that."

"I suspect they had help," Derec said. "And I bet we all know just who it was."

Over the comlink, he shouted, *Lucius*!

CHAPTER 8
REVOLUTION

Static.

A familiar type of static.

The static of robots in communication fugue. Many robots, from the sound of it.

Derec turned his head from side to side, trying to get a fix on them. There. Of course.

"They're in the Compass Tower."

Avery nodded. "Mandelbrot, get us some transportation."

Mandelbrot handed one of the other robots the flashlight and obediently moved off at a run down the street.

"They're using their comlinks again," Derec said while they waited. "That means they've decided to disregard direct orders."

"Why am I not surprised?" Avery flicked off the laser. The robot with the flashlight held it up overhead to make a pool of light with the humans in it.

Derec said, "It's my fault." He told Avery of his conversation with Lucius earlier in the day. "Evidently he decided he's best off if he doesn't consider anybody human."

"Evidently. Well, we'll soon fix that." Avery slapped the laser against his open palm.

They heard a soft whine, and moments later a dark shape drifted up the street toward them. The robot with the flashlight aimed it at the shape and it resolved into a truck with Mandelbrot at the controls. Mandelbrot brought it to a halt beside them and Avery and Derec climbed into the cab with him. The other robots climbed into the back, and they accelerated off toward the Compass Tower.

Sensing that his passengers didn't like speeding through the dark, Mandelbrot turned on the headlights. In their illumination Derec saw robots moving aimlessly along the sidewalks, as if unaware that anything had happened only a few blocks away.

"Good grief," Derec said. "Don't they care that half the city has been destroyed?"

Avery shook his head. "No curiosity, and they haven't received orders. Why they *haven't* is a mystery, but it's obvious they haven't."

As they drove on through the city, though, they began to notice more and more robots moving purposefully. "Looks like your new supervisors are getting things going again," Avery said.

Even as he spoke, the lights came back on. In the sudden brilliance, Derec nodded his agreement. "Looks like," he said. He twisted around in his seat and looked back the way they had come. A dark wedge still cut into the city's glow. He wondered how long it would take to erase that scar. In a normal city it would take years, but here? Maybe a day. Two at the outside.

● ● ●

The Compass Tower was the first building erected in a new robot city, and the only building to remain unchanged from day to day. As such, it housed the city's central memory, served as communications center, and also became a general meeting place. It was no surprise to find all seven of the city's supervisor robots there, nor, judging from the comlink static, to find them all standing immobile in the main conference room, locked in communication fugue. The three experimental robots were there as well.

This conference room was not a windowless closet. It was near the top of the building and had windows on three sides looking out over the city. Avery stood in the doorway a moment, surveying the scene, then raised the cutting laser up to aim at Lucius.

"Are you sure you want—?" Derec whispered, but Avery had already fired.

A shower of molten metal erupted from the robot's chest. Avery moved the point of destruction upward, toward its head and the positronic brain contained within, but the beam never reached its mark. Threatening Derec with a laser hadn't been enough to bring Lucius out of communication fugue before, but now that it was his own body under fire, Lucius became a blur of motion; a window suddenly grew a robot-sized hole in it, and he was gone.

Avery flicked the beam toward Adam, but he and Eve had already begun to move. Two more crashes and they were gone as well. Derec and Avery ran to the window in time to see three gigantic bird shapes disappear around the edge of the building.

The supervisor robots had also awakened, but they made no move to escape. Avery turned away from the window to face them and said, "All of you, deactivate. Now."

Six supervisors froze in place. The seventh took a halting step forward, said, "Please, I must—"

Avery fired his laser, this time at the head instead of the

chest. The robot fell to the floor, showering sparks. Avery swept the laser over the others, heads first, then methodically melted them all into puddles. When he was done he turned to the four robots Mandelbrot had brought with him. "You four are now supervisors. Access the central library for your duties."

"Yes, Master Avery," they said in unison. They were still for a moment, consulting the library via comlink, then as one being they turned and left the room to begin their new jobs.

Something about the sight sickened Derec. Seven cooling puddles of recently free robot stained the floor, and four new slaves moved off to take their places. And yet, and yet, what else could Avery have done? They had seen what happened when supervisors failed to perform their duties. The old supervisors might have been still usable—the one who had defied Avery's order might have been about to protest that he must see to restoring the city—but who could know? If that hadn't been what he'd been about to say, and if Avery hadn't fired when he had, they might have had ten renegade robots on their hands instead of three.

Three were bad enough. Time and again throughout the night, reports came in of the robots attempting to distract others from their duties. Avery had ordered hunter-seekers out to stop them, but that merely stopped the problem wherever there were hunters. He and Derec considered the idea of ordering all the city robots to arm themselves against the renegades, but rejected it after only a moment's thought. One didn't arm the peasants during a revolution.

Derec and Mandelbrot went back to the apartment and brought Ariel and Wolruf back to the Compass Tower, reasoning they would be safer there, guarded by hunter-seekers whose definition of "human" had been strengthened and refined to include the tower's four organic occupants, no matter who said otherwise. While he did that, Avery worked to strengthen the definition of human for all the city's robots, and thus the Second Law compulsion to obey.

Avery was a virtuoso at the computer. By the time Derec returned, he had finished the reprogramming and had even discovered the sequence of events that had led to the building's collapse.

"Look here," he said, motioning Ariel and Wolruf over to look at the screen as well. "I've got it displaying a priority map. This, down here at the bottom, is the original city programming." He pointed to a layer of blue near the bottom of the screen. Tiny blue lines rose from it to the next level, a green layer; some passed on through. "These lines are orders. The next level here, the green, is what you three put in when you were here last. Notice how your program stops nearly all the orders from the original layer. That's because you told the robots to quit expanding the city and to become farmers. They had a completely new instruction set. But look here." He pointed to a thick blue line extending up through the green layer. "You left in the part that lets the city metamorphose at random. Not a problem, but now this layer above that, the red one, is what the aliens—these Ceremyons of yours—put in. It's basically an order to ignore all the 'do' instructions in your level of programming, but keep all the 'don'ts.' See how every green line stops at the red boundary? All that gets through is the basic city maintenance that you left in, including the random metamorphosis. It worked just fine as long as the supervisors were in the circuit, because they also had verbal orders to keep things running, and they had enough volition to order things that weren't automatic anymore, but as soon as you take them out of the circuit, the whole thing falls apart."

He turned away from the screen and spoke directly to them. "So here's what happened: Building movement is essentially random, subject to supervisory override if the random number generator comes up with a ridiculous configuration. It doesn't happen often, about once a day, on the average. So without a supervisor to veto it, today's ridiculous building gets built. It turns out to be ridiculously tall. But the main power station doesn't have a supervisory order to generate more power for it, so when it starts to pull excessive current to lift all that mass, it trips the breaker. Power goes out. The original emergency programming has been blocked—twice, I point out with injured dignity—so without a supervisor's order, the auxiliary stations don't go on line. The building is unstable without power to hold it up, so it falls over. On the power station.''

"Oh," Derec said. One word can be expressive under the right circumstances.

Ariel said, "So we messed it up, that's what you're saying? It's our fault?"

Avery shook his head. "It's everyone's fault. Mine for not writing the original program to filter out the bad input before it reached the supervisors, yours for bypassing the emergency programming, the Ceremyons' for bypassing your bypass, the experimental robots for distracting the supervisors—take your pick. We're all in this together.''

"Even me?" Wolruf asked. The bandage across her forehead made her look a little like a pirate in a bad movie, and her toothy grin only added to the illusion.

"Even you. And yes, I've included you in the city robots' new definition of human. Basically I put them back to the old definition of anyone genetically similar to us, plus you. And I strengthened their devotion to duty as far as I can push it. That ought to keep them from listening to subversive arguments.''

It seemed to do the trick, all right, but their problems were far from over. The robot rebellion might have been quelled, but robots weren't this planet's only inhabitants.

The next morning the four "humans" were examining the wreckage when a black speck dropped down out of the sky, grew rapidly in size until it became visibly winged, and swooped in to stall to a stop just in front of them. It had the same shape as the three robots had when they returned from their discussion with the Ceremyons, but it was easy to tell that this was the real thing. The alien folded its wings and took a step closer until it stood before Ariel.

Ariel had been the one to initiate communication with the aliens before, and they had come to regard her as a leader among humans.

"You are Ariel," the one before her said in a high-pitched voice. "I am Sarco. We have met."

It was hard to see detail in the alien's body. It gained its nourishment from solar radiation, so it was an almost perfect black, reflecting not even the slightest amount of light back into its environment. The effect was like that of talking to a shadow, or to an eclipse. Only the white hook, with which it tethered itself for the night, and its two deep red eyes broke the darkness.

As far as Derec knew, Avery had never seen an alien before, but he played it cool. He studied the creature before them silently while Ariel replied, "Hello, Sarco. Good to see you again."

"I wish I could say the same, but unfortunately, I come with a complaint."

The alien's speech had improved considerably since Derec had last heard it. Before, it had sounded a little like someone with an Earth accent and a cold on top of it, but now it just sounded like it had a cold. It had evidently been practicing.

Derec could guess what the alien had come to complain about. Their society valued peace and quiet and maintaining the status quo; when he had dealt with them before, they had been ready to isolate the entire city under a force dome simply because they didn't like the heat it radiated. Now . . .

"You don't like buildings falling over in the night?" he asked facetiously.

"You are Derec. I do not."

Avery cleared his throat. "Neither do we."

Sarco turned his head, a motion evident only by the shifting position of the eyes and the hook. "We have not met."

"I am Doctor Avery. I designed the robots that built this city."

"I see. They have caused us considerable trouble. You neglected to include proper feedback mechanisms to limit their spread. We had to do that for you."

Avery hadn't expected such a direct accusation, but he took it gracefully. "I apologize. Causing you trouble wasn't my intention. When I sent them out, I didn't know you were here."

"Now you do. Will you remove them and their city?"

Avery frowned. "That would be difficult."

"But not impossible."

"No, not impossible. But definitely difficult, and probably unnecessary. Since the planet is already inhabited, my purpose for the robots can't be realized here, but I'm sure we can adapt them to be useful for you."

"We already attempted that. We need neither servants nor farmers."

"Well, what do you need?"

"We need nothing."

Avery snorted. "That's a little hard to believe. I'm offering you a whole city full of robots. Maybe you don't realize it, because their programming so far hasn't made much use of the capability, but the robots can change their shapes as readily as the city can. I can turn them into anything you like, and the city as well."

Sarco rustled his wings. "We have no need of a city full of robots, no matter what their shapes."

Avery shrugged. "Think about it. Derec tells me you guys are pretty bright. You should be able to come up with something you can use them for."

A tiny jet of flame appeared in the blackness below the alien's eyes. It was a sign of irritation, Derec knew. The flame went out, and Sarco said, "I will take the matter up in council. Perhaps we can think of something, so you will be spared the inconvenience of removing them." He stepped back, spread his wings, and with a powerful thrust leaped into the sky.

Avery watched him rise until he was out of sight, then shook his head and began walking along the collapsed building again. "Touchy, aren't they?" he asked of no one in particular.

The three renegade robots were nowhere to be found. They had stopped bothering the city robots when they realized that Avery's new programming was too tight for them to influence, but from that point on they effectively disappeared from sight. All of the city robots were under strict instructions to report the others if they were spotted, and to detain them if possible, but nothing came of it.

Derec tried the comlink, but was not surprised to receive no answer.

Within the space of the afternoon, the fallen building and its wreckage was nearly cleaned up. What city material that couldn't be immediately returned to the general inventory by simply instructing it to melt back into the street was hauled away to the fabrication site to be reprocessed, and the robots who had been damaged were repaired or replaced in the same way. By evening things were almost back to normal, right down to the medical robot who called the apartment just after dinner.

It was time for Ariel's checkup. She and Derec walked the short distance from the apartment to the rebuilt hospital alone. Wolruf sensed that they didn't need company, and Avery was already there in the hospital, working on another rat. They didn't talk. There was nothing to say. Either the embryo was developing normally again or it wasn't, and nothing they could say now would change it.

All four medical robots waited for them in the hospital. Derec held Ariel's hand while they set up their equipment around her, made their measurements, and studied the results. He knew from their silence what the outcome was long before they worked up the nerve to tell him.

"It isn't good," he said for them.

"That is correct. The neural folds have closed to form the neural tube, but there is no nerve tissue within it. It therefore seems likely that the baby will be born without a brain."

Ariel had been prepared to hear those words. She took a deep breath, let it out, and said, "Not this baby, it won't. Abort it."

The medical robot whom she had addressed backed up a pace and stammered, "I, I cannot do that."

"You can and you will. You just told me it won't have a brain. That means it won't be human, and it isn't human now. I want it out of me."

Slowly the robot said, "I have been programmed to consider anything with the proper genetic code to be human. No matter what deformities it may have, the embryo you carry is human by that definition."

"Well I'm changing the definition! I tell you it won't be, and I order you to abort it!"

The robot lost its balance, caught itself, and whispered, "I am sorry. I cannot." It tried to back away, but lost its balance again and toppled over, dead.

"Frost, I don't need this," Ariel muttered. She pointed

to another medical robot. "You. Listen to me. I—"

"Wait," Derec interrupted. "You'll get the same result with that one. Let me try changing its definition directly." He turned to the robot. "What is your designation?"

"I am Human Medical 3," the robot responded. Was that a trace of nervousness Derec heard in its voice? He'd as much as said he was going to reach into its brain and stir. The robot's Second Law obligation to follow human orders overrode his normal Third Law reluctance to allow it, especially now that Avery had reinforced the Second Law, but that didn't mean the robot couldn't still fear for its own existence.

"I won't harm you," Derec said for its benefit. *Central core. Update programming for Human Medical 3. Definition of human as follows: Any sentient organic being. This is not to include undeveloped beings.*

Acknowledged.

"Now, remove the embryo."

Human Medical 3 obediently reached toward a tray of instruments, but he stopped halfway. "I am experiencing . . . difficulty," he said in a halting voice.

"What's the problem? It's not human. You know it's not human. It has no chance of *becoming* human. Why can't you do it?"

"I—am programmed to care for human life. All such life. The oath of Hippocrates, which human doctors customarily take before beginning practice, specifically states that they will protect life 'from the moment of conception.' I am not bound by that oath, but it is a definition that I cannot ignore. Nor can I ignore the definition given every robot in the city yesterday by Doctor Avery. Now you add a third definition. It is the most recent one, but it is not the only one. My brain is an analog device, not digital; it is composed of positron pathways, each with a varying potential. Past potentials may weaken, but they never disappear. I cannot forget completely. I now have three conflicting potentials, and a life lies in the balance. Please, do not order me to take it.''

Derec fumed. Ariel had taken the news stoically, but it had to have been a blow for her. This arguing with the medical robots wasn't helping her a bit.

But it was obvious that ordering the robot to do it would only result in another dead robot, and that wouldn't help either.

''Cancel,'' he growled. Over the comlink, he sent, *Get me Avery*.

A moment later, he heard Avery's voice in his head. *What is it?*

We're in the exam room. Can you come down here?

How important is it? I'm in the middle of something here. It's important.

Avery sighed audibly. *All right. Be right there.*

''Avery's coming,'' Derec said to Ariel.

This time she didn't say anything snide. They both knew that Avery was a better roboticist than Derec; if anybody could convince a robot to abort a malformed embryo, he could.

But it appeared, after they explained the situation to him and he tried reprogramming and re-reprogramming the medical robots, that he couldn't do the job, either. The robots had had one too many redefinitions already, and they couldn't handle another. Avery sent the single survivor away in frustration.

Ariel had gotten up from the examination table and was now standing beside Derec, their arms around one another and her head resting against his shoulder. Avery looked up at her from his chair before the computer terminal where he had attempted the reprogramming and said, ''I'm sorry, my dear. It looks like you'll have to wait until we return to the original Robot City, or to Aurora.''

She nodded. Avery made to get up, but Ariel suddenly asked, "Can't we make another medical robot, one with a narrow definition of human from the start?"

Avery looked embarrassed. "I would have thought of that eventually." He turned back to the computer and began entering commands.

I have a question, a voice said in Derec's head.

Who is this?

Lucius.

Lucius! Where are you? Derec turned his head from side to side, trying to get a fix, but the impression was fuzzy, as if coming from a wide area. Were all three robots transmitting simultaneously, to mask their locations?

Nearby. I have been monitoring your efforts.

You've been spying on us?

You could call it that, yes. I prefer to think that I am continuing to research the Laws of Humanics. Before you abort the embryo Ariel carries, I need to ask a question that you may not have considered yet.

What question?

If the baby were to grow to term, then be provided with a positronic brain, would it then be human by your definition?

Derec's answer was instinctive, but no less correct for that. He shook his head violently. *No!*

"What's the matter?" Ariel asked.

"Lucius," Derec whispered. "He's talking to me."

"Is he—"

Why not?

"Just a minute." *It wouldn't be human because it wouldn't have a human brain, that's why not! That's the most important part.*

You seem quite certain of this.

Of course, I'm certain.

I am unconvinced.

This time it was Ariel who flinched, but it wasn't from anything Lucius said. She pulled away from Derec, shouting, "A rat!"

"Where?" Avery demanded.

She pointed toward the doorway, where a whiskered face was just peeking around the jamb.

"That's mine!" Avery shouted, jumping up from his chair and lunging for it. The face disappeared with a squeak.

"Stop!" Avery ran out into the corridor, but his footsteps ceased abruptly. Derec and Ariel heard him laugh. He came back into the room holding the rat by the tail. It didn't hang the way a rat normally did, with its feet spread wide. It looked more like a toy rat molded into a running position.

Avery laid it on its back on the exam table. "Stand up," he said to it, and it obediently rolled over and stood on its feet.

"Squeak."

The rat squeaked.

"Lift your right front paw."

The rat lifted its right front paw.

"I'd say we have our answer," he said to Derec. "You replace an organic brain cell by cell with a robot brain, and you still wind up with a robot." To the rat, he said, "Go wait for me in the lab." He pointed toward the door, and the rat jumped down from the table and scurried away through it.

I am convinced, Lucius sent.

You saw that?

I did.

How did you manage that?

If I reveal myself, will you promise that I will not be harmed?

Why should I promise you that?

Because I ask it as a friend. And I offer my help as a friend.

Your help in what?

I am now convinced that Ariel's wishes are right. I am willing to perform the operation if she wishes it.

You are? But you're not a doctor.

I can be within minutes.

He was right, of course. He could access the central library's medical files as easily as could any other robot.

Just a minute. Aloud, Derec said, "Lucius is here somewhere. He's making us an offer."

"What offer?" asked Ariel.

"He'll do the operation if we'll let him. In return he asks that we don't shoot at him anymore."

"Ridiculous!" Avery said with a snort. He looked toward Ariel, saw the determination on her face, and added, "Unless, of course, he and the other two agree to leave the rest of the robots in the city alone."

I promise that for all three of us, Lucius sent.

"He promises." To Ariel, Derec added, "But I don't know what that's worth. What do you think? I won't blame you if you don't trust him. We can make another robot do it."

She balled her fists and bit her lip, looked up at the ceiling, then shook her head. "I don't think he's dangerous. He's never hurt anyone intentionally. And I just want this whole business to be over with. So yes, tell him I'll trust him."

Derec was about to relay her words to Lucius, but he realized that he needn't bother. "Okay," he said aloud. "Come on out from wherever you're hiding."

There came a soft tearing sound, and a section of ceiling near the door peeled away to fall with a flop against the wall. It peeled off the wall as well, gathered into a lump on the floor, and quickly rose on two legs to become Lucius's familiar form.

● ● ●

Despite his other failings, Lucius made an excellent surgeon. Within a day, Ariel was up and walking around again, though still somewhat sore. Even so, she was far better off physically than mentally, for in that area neither Lucius nor anyone else could help her heal. Derec was the only one who could even begin to ease the torment she was going through, but he was feeling it just as strongly as she.

Had they done the right thing? Of course they had. They knew they had. Hadn't they?

As Derec struggled with his own feelings of guilt, he found himself appreciating Avery's position for the first time. What a load his father carried around with him, considering all he had done! With a background like his, just carrying on from day to day would be a continual struggle, especially with Derec there as a constant reminder of it.

No wonder Avery strove to keep busy. It kept his mind off his past. After an absolutely disastrous day spent moping around the apartment, both Derec and Ariel realized the wisdom of his strategy, and followed his example.

While Derec and Avery set to work preparing the city robots for their reprogramming to suit the Ceremyons, Ariel and Wolruf set out to meet with them to find out what they had decided they wanted. The meeting was easy to arrange; Lucius contacted Adam and Eve, who were back with the aliens again, and between them they settled on a time and place.

Ariel left for the meeting in relatively high spirits, but she returned with a puzzled frown.

"The Ceremyons want us to make philosophers out of the robots," she reported, slumping down in a chair and putting her hand to her forehead. "I told them that's not what robots were for, but they insisted. They said they've got a bunch of difficult philosophical questions that they haven't been able to work out, so their council decided to let the robots have a try at them."

"What are the questions?" Avery asked, looking up from his computer terminal.

"They didn't say. They said they wanted us to reprogram two robots for philosophy and let them see how well they work."

Derec and Avery looked at one another with eyebrows raised skeptically. Derec said, "I don't know, the original Wohler thought he was a philosopher, but I didn't think he was very profound."

"He was just spouting other people's philosophy," Ariel added. "He didn't come up with anything of his own."

"Of course he didn't," Avery said. "That's because he didn't do any cross-correlation." As Derec watched, Avery's skepticism disappeared, replaced by a fanatic gleam in his eye that Derec recognized. Avery saw the aliens' request as a challenge, and he intended to meet it. "He wasn't programmed to combine old information into new patterns, so all he could do was echo the thoughts of others. But if we give our robots the ability to compare and to generalize, and for working material load them up with all the philosophy texts in the central library, they'll be able to out-think these Ceremyons hands down. It won't be real *thinking*, but with a big enough library behind them, it'll be completely convincing to the user. Ha! It'll be easy." Avery turned back to the computer and began keying instructions furiously.

Without looking up, he said, "Get this city's Wohler unit up here to try it on. It should accept the new programming easier than just a random robot."

"You melted him along with the other supervisors," Derec reminded him.

"Oh. Well, then, have another one made."

Derec obediently contacted the central core and advised it that Avery wanted another Wohler.

"Here, you can help with the programming, too. Dig out

the code the supervisors use to reject crazy buildings, and see if you can modify it to filter out crazy thoughts. I'll work on the correlation routine."

With a smile and a shake of his head for Ariel's benefit, Derec got to work. Ariel and Wolruf stayed for a few minutes, but soon became bored and left. Lucius stayed, standing silently behind Derec and Avery where he could see what either of them did.

They spent the better part of the afternoon on the project, but they were ready by the time a new golden-hued robot presented itself at the door.

"I am Wohler-10," the robot said.

Avery looked up, rubbed his eyes, and said, "Good. Scan this." He handed Wohler a memory cube, which the robot took in its right hand. The hand flowed until it completely enveloped the cube, then after a few seconds returned to normal. Wohler gave the cube back to Avery.

"What is the relationship between free will and determinism?" Avery asked him.

"Determinism is necessary for free will, but not the reverse," the robot answered without hesitation.

"Did you think that up just now, or was it already in memory?"

"It was already in memory."

"Hmm. How does free will differ from freedom, and how does that difference affect a robot's behavior?"

Wohler hesitated slightly this time before saying, "Free will is the ability to act upon desires. Freedom is the ability to use free will indiscriminately. For practical purposes, a robot has neither. I can elaborate if you wish."

"No, that's fine. Was that your thought this time?"

"It was a correlation from existing definitions, but it did not exist previously in the data bank."

"Good. What is reality?"

"I quote: 'Reality is that which, when you cease to believe in it, does not go away.' Source: Phillip K. Dick, twentieth century author, Earth. I have on file seventy-three other definitions, but that one seems most logical.''

Avery grinned at Derec and spread his hands. ''One out of three responses are original. That's a pretty good average among philosophers. I think he'll do.''

Lucius made a humming sound, a robotic clearing of the throat. ''May I ask a question?''

Avery frowned. He obviously still didn't trust the renegade robot, but with a shrug, he said, ''Fire away.''

Lucius turned to face Wohler. ''What is a human?''

Wohler hesitated even longer than before. At last he said, ''That definition depends upon your point of view.''

Avery burst into laughter. ''He's a philosopher, all right! Come on, let's fix up another one and give them to the Ceremyons tomorrow.''

They chose a regular city robot for the second philosopher, testing him thoroughly to make sure that his answers were the same as the brand-new Wohler's. His experiences in the city and his previous reprogrammings didn't seem to affect his responses at all. They arranged a meeting through Lucius, and this time they all went to present the philosopher robots to the aliens.

They met at the edge of the spaceport farthest from the city, a spot no doubt chosen by the aliens to communicate their displeasure with the city and its inhabitants.

There were two of the living silhouettes at the meeting this time, as well as two alien-looking but obviously robotic companions: Adam and Eve. The robots ignored the humans, and the humans returned the courtesy. Sarco ignored the robots as well, but, realizing that humans couldn't distinguish one alien from another, he introduced himself again, then introduced his companion, Synapo, whom all but Avery had already met the first time they had been to Ceremya.

"And these are the philosophers?" Synapo asked dubiously. "I believe I recognize this one. It directed the killing of two of my people when this city first began growing here. It is a most unpleasant robot."

Derec had forgotten about that incident. It had happened because the robots didn't see the aliens as human, and were following the simplest procedure to get them out of the way. It was a stupid mistake then, and Derec's decision to use a Wohler model for a philosopher was a stupid mistake now. Wars had been fought over lesser matters.

"This is a different robot," he said, trying to smooth over the unintended insult. "The old Wohler was inactivated."

"A wise decision," Synapo said. The alien looked to its companion, receiving an eyeblink and a rustling of its wings in response. That was evidently the Ceremyon equivalent of a shrug, because Synapo said, " Well, then, to the test. Sarco, do you wish to ask the first question, or shall I?"

"The honor is yours," Sarco said.

Synapo bobbed down and up again in a gesture no doubt meant as an acceptance of Sarco's courtesy. "Very well. The new Wohler, then. I ask you this: What is the value of argument?"

Wohler folded his arms across his chest, a gesture Derec had taught him, and said, "The value of argument is that it allows two opposing views to be expressed, along with supporting evidence for each, so that an examination of the evidence can then lead to a determination of the more correct of the two views."

"A reasonable answer. And you, the other robot. Your name?"

"Plato."

"Plato. What is your answer to the same question?"

"It must, of course, be the same answer."

A tiny flame shot out from the darkness of Synapo's face. Sarco said, "Why must it be?"

"It is the correct answer."

"Then *apply* that answer to the discussion at hand!"

Plato looked at Sarco, then shifted its eyes to look help-lessly at Derec. "I must disagree with a correct answer?"

Synapo's flame winked out. "Of course you must!" he said. "That is the root of philosophical debate. If we all agreed, we could learn nothing."

Plato tried. He said, "Then I . . . then argument has no value. It is a pointless waste of energy. The correct answer should be obvious to all."

"Wrong!"

"Of course it is wrong!" Plato said desperately. "You told me to disagree with a correct answer!"

"That did not mean you had to give an incorrect one. You are not a philosopher. Dr. Avery, these robots are useless to us."

"Wrong," said Wohler. "We are useless to you in our present form."

Synapo jetted flame again, but Sarco jiggled up and down in obvious amusement. "It caught you!" the alien hooted.

Synapo's eyes shifted to the robot. "I stand corrected. You are useless to us in your present form. Perhaps in another form you would not be useless. Dr. Avery, what else can these robots do?"

"What do you want them to do?" Avery asked in return.

"Philosophize, but that seems too much to ask. Sarco, do you have another suggestion?"

"You know I do," Sarco replied. His eyes shifted to meet Avery's. "At our council meeting, I suggested that the robots be used as musicians. It was my thought that each of us could be attended by a personal musician who could play melodies to fit our individual moods."

"That's simple," Avery said. "They can do that without modification."

"Unlikely," Sarco said. "Our music consists of modulated hyperwave emissions."

"Okay, then," Avery said with a nod, "we'll need to give them hyperwave transmitters. And you'll have to teach them some of your songs."

"That can be done. Synapo?"

"Very well. My suggestion came to nothing; we'll see how yours fares. When will the robots be modified?"

"I can have them back to you by tomorrow," Avery said.

"We will be here." Synapo backed away, gave a running hop, and was airborne. Sarco followed, and Adam and Eve, who had been silently flanking them all along, also turned to go.

"Wait a minute," Derec said. "I want to talk to you."

"What do you wish to say?" the one on the left asked in Adam's voice.

"Why don't you come back with us?"

"We do not wish to."

"Why not? You can have the same deal we made Lucius. Peaceful coexistence while you figure out your definition of human."

"We are working on that definition with the Ceremyons. In fact, at this point we believe them to be more human than you."

"Because they don't ask you to do anything," Ariel put in.

"You have a clear understanding of the situation," the robot replied.

Avery shook his head. "Stay with them forever, for all I care. Good riddance. Come on, Wohler, Plato. Let's see if we can give you two rhythm."

They could, but that, it seemed, was not enough. It came close, closer than their first attempt to please the aliens, but on the morning of the third day after the trial, Lucius received a message from his counterparts that the aliens wanted to meet with the 'self-named humans' one more time.

They took transport booths out to the edge of the spaceport again. Sarco and Synapo were already waiting for them by the time they arrived, along with Adam and Eve and the musician robots as well.

Wohler was still recognizable by his gold color, but that was the only way to tell him from the other three robots. All had taken on the Ceremyon form.

The alien on the right stepped forward and said, "I am Sarco. These robots are not musicians."

"What's the problem this time?" Avery asked with a sigh.

"They are nothing more than elaborate recording and playback devices with the limited ability to improvise on a theme. In all the time they have been with us, not once has either of them been able to create a completely new piece of music."

"Well, not quite," amended Synapo. "They are able to produce random variations, which are new."

Sarco snorted flame. "I said 'new piece of music,' not just new noise."

"Sarco is a music lover," Synapo explained. "He is greatly disappointed."

Avery nodded. "All right. Let's get one thing straight. Twice now you've asked me to give you robots with creative minds. I've tried to accommodate you, but I think you're missing the point. Robots aren't supposed to be used for creativity. That's *our* job. Robots were made for the drudge work, for servants and laborers and all the other tasks that you need to have done in order to keep a society going but that nobody wants to do."

Sarco said, "Our society exists without such drudge work, as you call it."

"Then you don't need robots."

"Which is precisely what I told you at our first meeting."

Avery threw up his hands in defeat. "All right. Forget it. We'll take them off your hands. I was just trying to be helpful."

The irony of it was, Derec thought, Avery really *was* trying to be helpful. It was almost as if he wanted to prove to himself that he could still do it. And here the aliens were telling him that the only way he could help was to take his toys and go home.

"May I ask what you intend to do with them?" Synapo asked.

"What does it matter? They won't bother you anymore."

"I am curious."

"All right, since you're curious; I'll probably order them to self-destruct."

Synapo and Sarco exchanged glances. The robots did so as well.

"That would be a great waste," Synapo said.

"Waste? You just said they weren't any good to you. With the planet already occupied, they aren't any good to me, either. If there's no use for them, then how can it be a waste to get rid of them?"

"They represent a great degree of organization."

"Who cares? Organization doesn't mean anything. An apple has more complex organization than a robot. What matters isn't how sophisticated it is, but how much it costs you to produce. These robots are self-replicating; you can get a whole city from one robot if you've got the raw materials, so their cost is effectively zero. That's how much we lose if we get rid of them: nothing."

"But the robots lose. You forget, they are intelligent beings. Not creative, granted, but still intelligent. Perhaps too intelligent for the purpose for which you use them, if this is your attitude toward them."

"They're machines," Avery insisted.

"So are we all," Sarco said. "Biological machines that have become self-aware. And self-replicating as well. Do you maintain that our value is also zero, that we need not be concerned with individual lives, because they are so easy to replace?"

Avery took a deep breath, working up to an explosive protest, but Ariel's response cut the argument from under him.

"No," she whispered. "They're all important." She turned to Avery, and her voice grew in intensity as she said, "We just went through all this. Didn't we learn anything from it? Derec and I aborted our own baby because it was going to be born without a brain. Without that, it was just a lump of cells. Doesn't that tell us something? Doesn't that tell us the brain is what matters?"

Lucius said to Derec, "You told me that adding a robot brain to the baby at birth would not have made it human."

Ariel looked surprised, and Derec realized she hadn't been in on that conversation. Even so, it only slowed her down for a moment. "That's right," she said. "It wouldn't have. It would have been a robot in a baby's body, and we didn't want a baby robot. But the one question you didn't ask was whether or not we would have aborted it if it was *already* as intelligent as a robot, and the answer is no. We wouldn't have, because even a robot is self-aware. Self-awareness is what matters."

"You are more civilized than we thought," Synapo said.

"We try." Ariel reached out a hand toward Wohler. "Come on," she said. "I owe you a favor. The original Wohler lost his life saving me from my own stupidity; the least I can do is save his namesake."

The golden-hued robot alien stepped closer to her, its features twisting from Ceremyon form to humanoid form as it moved, until by the time it stood before her, it was again a normal, Avery-style robot. One of the three others also made the change, becoming the philosopher Plato, for-merly Transport Systems Coordinator 45.

Synapo shifted his weight, as if unused to standing so long. "In light of our discussion, I will repeat my question. What do you intend to do with them?"

"Send them back to the original Robot City, I guess," Avery said. "There's room for them there."

"And the city itself?" Synapo tilted his head to indicate the one before them, not the original. "It is self-aware also, is it not?"

"To a very limited degree," Avery replied. "It's aware of its own existence, but just enough so it can obey the same three laws the robots do. Everything else; the metamorpho-sis, the growth, the coordination, is all straight program-ming."

"Then you may leave the city, if you wish."

"What will you do with it? I didn't think you had any more use for a city than you have for robots."

"We don't. But if you remove all but its most basic programming, then it need not remain a city."

Avery looked back over his shoulder at the grand collec-tion of tall spires, pyramids, geometric solids, and elevated walkways connecting them all. Sunlight glinted off one face of the Compass Tower. Tiny specks of motion on the walk-ways were robots going about their assigned duties, keeping the city functioning. Derec, watching him, could read Avery's thoughts as well as if he'd heard them by comlink.

How can they not need all that?

Avery turned back to the Ceremyons. Shadows with red eyes waited for him to speak. "All right," he said at last. "What do I care what you do with it? It's yours."

"Thank you."

"You'll need some kind of control mechanism," Avery pointed out.

"We have already developed that capability," Sarco said.

"Oh?"

"Our technology is not as obvious as yours, but that is only because we choose not to let its presence spread unchecked."

Avery was working himself up to an explosive reply, but he got no chance. Before he could speak, the aliens bobbed up and down once each, turned, and took wing. This time Adam and Eve followed immediately. Lucius watched them rise up into the sky, and as he watched, his arms flattened toward wing shape and his body shrank in size to allow more bulk for the wings. He took a couple of clumsy steps, flapped his wings, and completed the transformation in the air.

"Hey!" Derec shouted. "Where are you going?"

Lucius circled around, swooped low, and as he swept past, shouted, "I will return!" Then with powerful strokes he flew off after his two siblings.

"Better return soon, or you'll be stranded here," Avery muttered, turning away and heading back toward the transport booths and the city. Without looking back to see if anyone followed, he said, "Wohler! Get our ship ready for space."

The robots didn't travel by ship. Under Avery's direction the city built a new Key center, a factory in which the tiny individual jump motors he called Keys to Perihelion were manufactured, and within hours each robot in the city had his own Key, its destination preset for the original Robot City. On Avery's command, they all formed up in a line, began marching down the main avenue toward the Compass Tower, and as they reached the intersection directly in front of it, jumped.

Their motion was hypnotic, and it lasted for hours. There had been a lot of robots in the city.

"So why don't we just use Keys to go back home ourselves?" Derec asked.

"Because I don't trust them."

"What do you mean, you don't trust them? You invented them yourself, didn't you?"

"An inventor is supposed to trust everything he makes?"

Wolruf, who had just keyed in an order on the automat for something Derec didn't recognize, looked at her plate with theatrical suspicion. Derec laughed.

"I'd use one in an emergency," Avery went on, "and I've done so in the past, but not without apprehension. If you think getting lost by jumping too far in a ship is dangerous, imagine it with just a key."

"You mean some of those robots won't make it home?" Ariel asked, shocked.

Avery rolled his eyes. "Of course they'll make it home, eventually. Some of them just may have to spend a day or two floating in space while they wait for the Key to recharge for a second shot at it. No problem for a robot, but a little more difficult for a human."

Derec felt a chill run up his back. He and Ariel had used the Keys half a dozen times, once jumping all the way from Earth's solar system to Robot City. They had thought they were in perfect safety all the while, but now to find out they weren't . . .

What did it matter, after the fact? It shouldn't have mattered at all, but it did to Derec. It filled him with anger. Too many things were not what they seemed. It sometimes felt as if the universe were playing a game with him, challenging him to figure it out before a wrong assumption killed him. Well, he no longer felt like playing.

But it wasn't a game you could quit. You could only lose. Eventually something—a mistake, a wrong assumption, bad luck—would happen to you and you would lose the game.

Derec seemed to be losing it in pieces. First his family, then his memory, then his chance to start a family of his own. Now he could feel his self-confidence starting to go as well. How much more could he afford to lose?

And what was the point in that kind of existence, anyway? Perhaps Wohler and Plato knew, but Derec doubted it. He doubted that the Ceremyons knew, either. That was no doubt one of their unanswered questions they had wanted the robots to answer for them.

He was looking out the window in his bleak mood when he noticed three silver-gray Ceremyon forms dropping down out of the sky toward the city. They drew nearer, dipping and weaving in the unstable air over the buildings, until they fluttered to a stop on the balcony. Derec went to the door to let them in.

Lucius went through the transformation to humanoid form and stepped through the doorway. Adam and Eve followed him. Once inside, Lucius said to Derec, "We bring information which you may find useful. And we come to ask a favor in return."

"What favor?"

"First let us tell you our information. The woman whom the Ceremyons told us of earlier, the one whom you believe may be your mother and our creator; we have finally found where she has gone."

Derec had thought he was immune to sudden enthusiasm, so blue had been his mood only moments ago, but the adrenaline dumped into his bloodstream when he heard Lucius's words burned that away instantly. Here was a chance to regain a part of what the universe had taken from him.

"Where?"

"She has gone to the planet of the Kin, where Adam was born."

"How long ago?"

"Just before we arrived here."

Derec looked away out the window, down at the line of robots queuing up for their trip to a home they had never seen. He felt a kinship with each of them, for he knew what their feelings were at this moment, if indeed they had feelings. He turned around to face Avery. "We've got to go after her. I remember what you said, but I still want to find her."

Avery's brow furrowed in thought, then he said, "Oddly enough, so do I. I have a few words on the subject of robotics to say to the creator of these three."

Derec sighed in relief. He had expected a struggle. "Ariel?" he asked. "What about you? You don't have to go if you don't want to. We can keep a few robots here, have them build you another ship before they—"

Ariel cut him off. "I want to be with you. I'll go where you go. Besides, I don't want to go home just yet. Not until I sort out a few things in my mind."

Wolruf waited until Derec looked over at her, then said, "Somebody's got to keep 'u out of trouble. Count me in."

"And now we come to the favor we ask of you," Lucius said. "We would like to come with you as well."

"To find your creator?"

"Yes. Failing that, we would study the Kin to see if they can offer us more insight into the question of humanity."

"Why should we take you along?" Avery asked. "You're nothing but trouble. You don't follow orders, and twice now you've almost killed us because of it."

"We would promise to consider more carefully the consequences of our actions. We will follow your orders when they seem reasonable. We would, in short, consider you our friends, and act accordingly."

"Friends. Ha."

"It might interest you to know that we now have three laws which we feel cover the interactions between sentient beings and their environment. The first is the Ceremyons' law: All beings will do that which pleases them most. The second is the law we formulated on our journey here: A sentient being may not harm a friend, or through inaction allow a friend to come to harm. The third, which we have formulated after watching the interaction among you four and among the Ceremyons, is this: A sentient being will do what a friend asks him to, but a friend may not ask him to do unreasonable things. With that in mind, we ask that you allow us to travel with you, as friends.''

''Your 'laws' seem awfully vague,'' Avery growled.

''Sentient beings are vague. We believe that to be an inherent quality of sentience.''

''Ha. Maybe so.'' Avery glared at the robots a moment longer, then shook his head. ''What the hell, it'll make for an interesting trip. Okay. You're on.''

''We thank you.''

''Yeah, yeah. Get on board. The ship leaves as soon as we get there. And hey, 'friends,' I've got three bags in my room. Since you're already headed that way, why don't you each grab one on the way out?''

Lucius glanced over to Adam and Eve. They returned his glance, then they all three looked momentarily at Avery. At last Lucius nodded. ''We would be glad to,'' he said.

Derec took one last look at their apartment as the transport booth whisked him away for the last time. It was already just one among hundreds of elaborate but now completely empty buildings in a city all but devoid of life. When he and the others crossed its bounds at the spaceport, it would be just that.

The city robots were already gone. The city itself had stopped its transformations, was now locked into the shape it had held when Avery cancelled its program. The only motion besides their transport booths were the half-dozen Ceremyons circling overhead, watching. Waiting.

The booths slowed to a stop at the terminal building. Their ship, the *Wild Goose Chase*, waited only a short walk away, repaired and gleaming in the sunlight. Derec took Ariel's hand and together they walked toward it, enjoying the warmth of the sun and the smell of unfiltered air one last time before boarding.

A soft whisper of movement behind them made them stop and look around, just in time to see the last of the city buildings dissolve. The spaceport terminal building was the only structure left; all the others had melted down into a pool of undifferentiated city material the moment they had crossed the boundary. Tiny ripples spread across the silvery surface, like ripples in a lake but propagating much faster in the denser liquid. There was a hush of expectation in the air; then a jet of silver sprayed upward at an angle, arching over to splash back into the surface nearly halfway across the lake. The beam must have been a meter thick, Derec supposed.

Where it met the surface, a disturbance arose, and a familiar sight climbed back up the beam: the splashing, outward-spraying point of contact between the downfalling jet and a new one spraying upward at the same angle from the same point. The meeting point reached the top and stopped there, a vertical sheet of liquid silver spraying out from what appeared to be a solid arch. The noise of it splashing back into the lake was the roar of a waterfall. Derec recognized in an instant what it was: a copy on an enormous scale of the fountain in the entryway to their apartment in the original Robot City, the fountain he called ''Negative Feedback.''

How had the Ceremyons learned of that? he wondered, but the answer came almost immediately. Lucius had no doubt told them about it, possibly to ask them its significance. Derec *had* ordered him to think about it, after all.

He turned to see the amusement on Ariel's face, and found himself grinning as well.

''Think they're trying to tell us something?'' he asked.

GARDENER ROBOT: Gardener robots tend the pocket parks and other plant life in Robot City. Like the traditional gardeners of Earth, they tend to remain in the background, ignored by passing humans or other robots.

While all robots are bound by the First Law to protect human life, these have a particular sensitivity to life in general, since their taste is to work with ornamental plants. More than agricultural robots, gardeners tend to see each plant as individual and alive.

LUCIUS'S LABORATORY: One of many such laboratories used in his project for creating human beings, Lucius's laboratory is reminiscent of a typical mad-scientist's lair. Bubbling vats, interconnected glassware, and cages filled with small animals contrast with organic chemistry analyzers, microscopes, and gleaming robot technicians, but all are necessary tools for the creation of life from simple organic molecules.

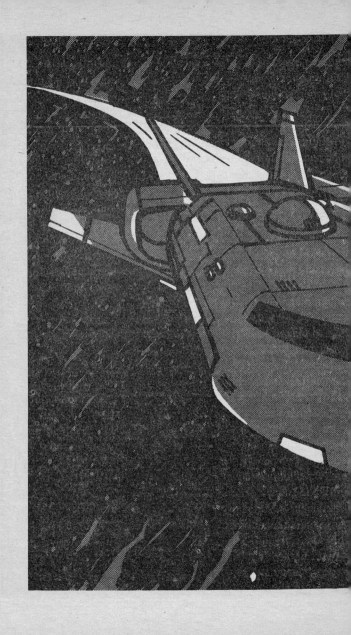

THE *WILD GOOSE CHASE*: So named by Dr. Avery, only partly in jest, the *Wild Goose Chase* is one of the cellular spaceships Derec ordered built for his and Ariel's use. Constructed of Robot City building material, it can assume whatever shape is optimal at the time, becoming a winged craft for ascent and landing and whatever shape most easily accommodates its passengers during flight.

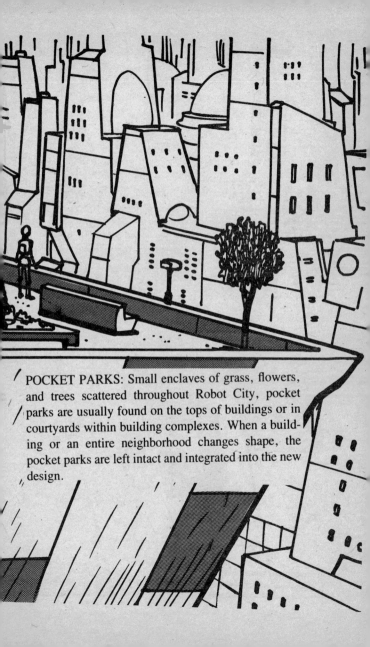

POCKET PARKS: Small enclaves of grass, flowers, and trees scattered throughout Robot City, pocket parks are usually found on the tops of buildings or in courtyards within building complexes. When a building or an entire neighborhood changes shape, the pocket parks are left intact and integrated into the new design.

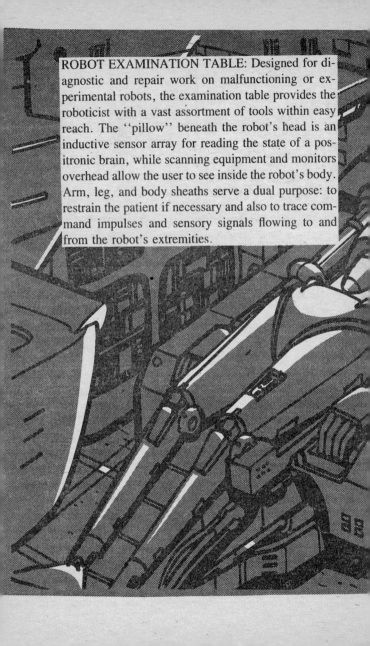

ROBOT EXAMINATION TABLE: Designed for diagnostic and repair work on malfunctioning or experimental robots, the examination table provides the roboticist with a vast assortment of tools within easy reach. The "pillow" beneath the robot's head is an inductive sensor array for reading the state of a positronic brain, while scanning equipment and monitors overhead allow the user to see inside the robot's body. Arm, leg, and body sheaths serve a dual purpose: to restrain the patient if necessary and also to trace command impulses and sensory signals flowing to and from the robot's extremities.

JERRY OLTION

Jerry Oltion is the author of *Frame of Reference*, a novel about a generation-style starship that isn't. He is currently at work on *Paradise Passed*, an interstellar colony novel. His short stories appear frequently in *Analog* magazine, two of them winning first and third places in the 1987 Readers' Choice Awards. His stories have also been nominated for the Nebula Award.